*T*he
*U*nderground
*S*tream

Previous novels by Velda Johnston

Flight to Yesterday
The Man at Windmere
The Girl on the Beach
The House on Bostwick Square
The Fatal Affair
Shadow Behind the Curtain
The Crystal Cat
Voice in the Night
The Other Karen
The Fateful Summer
The Stone Maiden
A Presence in an Empty Room
The People from the Sea
The Silver Dolphin
The Hour Before Midnight
The Etruscan Smile
Deveron Hall
The Frenchman
A Room with Dark Mirrors
The House on the Left Bank
I Came to the Highlands
The White Pavilion
Masquerade in Venice
The Late Mrs. Fonsell
The Mourning Trees
The Face in the Shadows
The People on the Hill
The Light in the Swamp
The Phantom Cottage
I Came to the Castle
A Howling in the Woods
House Above Hollywood
Along a Dark Path

The Underground Stream

VELDA JOHNSTON

St. Martin's Press   New York

This one too is for Jeanne Waring, along with my gratitude for her aid and advice.

One

One of the strangest things about that house, it seems to me now, is that it did not look in the least strange. True, it was old. Probably it had been built around 1810. But in a village filled with eighteenth- and nineteenth-century houses, mere age was no distinction. Nor was it even a good example of its period. A tall brown shingledown with white shutters, it had been built on the least costly plan possible: four rooms up and four down. Except for its peaked roof, its shape was that of an upended packing crate.

But if what happened to me in that house was in any sense real, rather than a product of my emotional state, then that ordinary-looking structure was a strange dwelling indeed.

I had never expected even to see that house, let alone enter it. In fact, I had never expected to find myself in Hampton Harbor. For more than half of my twenty-four years, the very mention of that village far out on eastern Long Island had been enough to fill me with a chill unease. And yet there I was that afternoon early last July, piloting the small car I had rented in Manhattan that morning along narrow, tortuous streets, some with cracked sidewalks, some with no sidewalks, but all filled with the shifting light and shadow of sun filtered through breeze-stirred branches.

It was because of Beth Garmish that I had ventured to this town. About a week earlier she had telephoned me at my apartment on West Eighty-seventh Street, her voice hoarse from weeping.

"Gail, Pete and I have split up."

Pete was Peter Garmish, the young abstract painter she had married less than a year ago. "For good? Isn't there a chance that—"

"No chance at all. He's gone back to that woman sculptor he used to live with." Her voice rose to a wail. "She's *forty*. If I'd known in time that what Pete really wants is a mother—"

"Beth, I'm so sorry. Is there anything I can—"

"Yes! You can come out here and spend the rest of the summer with me. You know the crazy way Pete has with money. He gave the owner the whole summer's rent in advance. So you might as well have the benefit of it."

With dismay I looked through my none-too-clean windows at the fire escapes zig-zagging down the rear of a building that faced the next street. "Beth, I couldn't."

"Why not? A few weeks out here would be just the thing after your—illness." I was sure that she had almost said breakdown. "It's a fascinating old town. More than a hundred years ago, you know, this was a whaling port."

I knew. My ancestor, Samuel Fitzwilliam, the one I had found out about the summer I was eleven, had owned whaleships. "Beth, I just couldn't."

"But why?"

I could not tell her why. Aside from the woman shrink they had assigned to me at the Morse-Whitlow Clinic here in Manhattan, I had talked to only one person, a man, about what had happened in a town called Hampton Harbor a century and a half ago. And I had come to regret bitterly telling *him*. "Beth, it just seems too much of an effort."

2

"That's apathy talking. Once you're out here you'll enjoy it. There's so much to do, beaches and galleries and antique shops—"

When I did not answer she said, "Look, Gail. Now that I've lost Pete, you and I are in the same boat. Let's say to hell with men and chop off the hands of any bastard who tries to climb aboard."

Her tear-roughened voice went on. Only half listening, I looked through the smudged windows. There was no real reason why I should spend the rest of the summer in New York, my heels sinking in heat-softened asphalt at street intersections, when I could be enjoying salt-laden breezes. My boss at the advertising firm of Horton and Jedlow had told me not to come back to work until September, "and not even then if you don't feel up to it."

What was more, that shrink had told me that I must not let my life be dictated by what had happened to my immediate forebears, let alone my great-great-great-grandfather.

My last day at the clinic, seated with me in my small but pleasant room, all cheery chintz and Swedish modern furniture, Dr. Helen Vorney had said, "Remember, Gail, there is no such thing as a completely normal human being. Anyone will break if subjected to sufficient stress. You withstood quite a lot before you broke, and you've made a swift recovery. So put all this behind you and get on with your life."

What, I wondered, would she say if I telephoned her about Beth's offer? Probably she would say I would be a fool to spend July and August in this apartment, with its old air conditioner that never reduced the temperature below a soggy seventy-eight degrees. I couldn't be sure, of course, because I didn't know where to call her. The last time she had phoned me, "just to find out how things are going," she had told me that she, along with almost every psychiatrist and psychoanalyst in New York, would be vacationing on Cape Cod. Nevertheless, I was quite sure she would advise me to take up Beth's offer.

"Gail, are you listening to me?"

"Yes."

"Then how about it?"

"I'll come."

"Oh, Gail!" Her voice broke. "I don't know how I could have stood it out here alone. And it would be even worse back in the apartment with Pete not there." She swallowed audibly and then went on in a more controlled tone, "I didn't bring much bed linen from the city. So could you bring your own sheets and blankets?"

"Of course."

"And some decent table silver. Knives and forks and spoons come with the place, but they look like they'd been used in an army field kitchen during the Civil War."

"All right."

And so early the next morning I had rented a gray Nissan from an agency far over on the West Side, driven it back to my apartment to load it with my suitcase, bed clothes, and tableware, and then headed east through heavy traffic to the expressway. As I drove, all but a trace of my doubt gave way to anticipation. Even though the Hamptons were only 125 miles from New York, I had never visited them. During my childhood and adolescent years I had vacationed on the New Jersey shore, first with my father and mother, and then, after their divorce, with my mother and my Great Aunt Louise. During my college years at Barnard, and later on at Horton and Jedlow, I had resisted all suggestions that I join one of the groups of singles who rented Hampton houses for the season. Still, I knew quite a lot about the Hamptons. Each Monday during the summer my colleagues would come to work sporting deepened tans and stories about romantic adventures among the dunes or in some bar or night club.

Following the directions Beth had given me over the phone, I circled the tall flagpole in Bridgehampton and then followed the road to Hampton Harbor. I drove down a wide street where cars were parked at an angle before solid rows of brick or wooden buildings, some of which appeared to date from the mid-nineteenth century. At the foot of the street, where a wharf stretched out into the blue, sun-spangled bay, I turned right and then, still following Beth's directions, right again. Finally I stopped before the house she had described to me, a small white Cape Cod cottage with a marigold-bordered brick walk leading up to a green door.

Somehow I had expected to see Beth—her pretty freckled face in its frame of short red curls—peering at me from the front window. But the curtains did not stir. And for several seconds after I rapped the brass knocker against the green door, there was no response.

Then the door opened. Beth stood there, her face holding a strange mixture of guilt, embarrassment, and rapturous joy.

"Hello, Gail." She opened the door wider.

Looking over her shoulder I saw the reason for her joy, and I suppose her guilty embarrassment too. Pete Garmish stood there, a sheepish look on his face. As always, I was struck by the fact that his hair and beard were the same shade as Beth's curls. Somehow the beard did not add any years to his appearance. On the contrary, with his round blue eyes and full-lipped mouth, he looked like a young boy who had pasted on a beard as a joke.

Beth said unnecessarily, "Pete came back." She opened the door still wider. "Come in."

I followed them down a short hall and then into a small living room. Like most summer cottage living rooms, it appeared to have been furnished exclusively with items picked up at yard sales. Beth said, "You must be thirsty. What will you have to drink?"

"Nothing, thanks." A premonitory anger was speeding my heartbeat. "I get the feeling you are pressed for time. If you have something to tell me, why not say it right now?"

"Oh, Gail!" Her smile looked more embarrassed than ever, but joy still shone in her eyes. "We *are* in sort of a hurry. Pete and I are going to fly to Paris for a month or so."

"On the night plane," Pete said. No need to ask whose idea

this impromptu trans-Atlantic jaunt had been. He looked even more like a small boy in a paste-on beard.

"That sounds great," I answered. "But what about me? Will it be all right if I just move my things in and—"

"Oh, Gail!" Beth cried. "We tried to phone you this morning, but I guess you'd already left. You see—"

"I'll tell her," Pete said. "I told you I would take the responsibility. I got a refund from the landlady for the rest of the summer's rent. She knows someone who wants the place badly. And we wouldn't be able to make this Paris trip without that refund."

So I had rented a car and driven all this way to a town I had never wanted even to see, only to find that I would not have a roof over my head.

"We're terribly sorry about it," Beth said, still with that joy shining in her eyes.

There are few things harder than having to hide what you regard as justifiable anger. And it's even harder when you feel called upon to express instead a congratulatory warmth.

"It's all right. And I'm awfully happy for both of you."

"If you wanted to spend a few days in Hampton Harbor," Beth said, "there's a nice motel near the foot of Main Street."

"Perhaps," I said. "Or perhaps I'll just turn around and drive back to Manhattan. I'll think about it."

A few minutes later, holding tight to my temper, I kissed them both and said goodbye. As I drove away along the narrow street I tried to tell myself that I really was glad that Pete and Beth were back together. But I could not help feeling almost childishly disappointed. Facing down my demons, I had accepted an invitation to spend the rest of the summer here, only to find the invitation withdrawn.

Then I realized that that did not mean I must return to New York or that, if I remained here, I would have to stay in a motel. Surely not all the rentals on eastern Long Island were gone.

Suddenly I found that I very much wanted to stay here, right in this town. I wanted to prove to myself that the memory of my

6

Great Aunt Louise's drunken words, spoken on the porch of that New Jersey summer cottage more than a dozen years before, had lost much of its power to influence me.

If rents weren't too staggering, I could afford a house for the next two months. The advertising agency had not suspended my salary. Besides, I still had money left from the sale of the large, gloomy apartment my mother had owned.

I drove even more slowly than before, looking for "For Rent" signs. How attractive these old houses were, some quite imposing with their pillared porticos, others small and charming, with gossip benches facing each other on tiny porches. Occasionally I saw a slovenly house, its grass weed-grown and its paint shabby. But most of them appeared well tended, their smooth lawns set with flower beds. And I loved the street names—Accord Street, and Patriot Street, and, one right after the other, four streets named Matthew, Mark, Luke, and John. I had not as yet encountered Monroe Street, or if I had I had not been aware of it.

Monroe Street was where my great-great-great-grandparents had lived.

"The Monster," my Great Aunt Louise had said. She smelled of gin and vermouth. In the sunset light striking under the porch roof of that little New Jersey cottage, her lined and heavily made-up face had a smeared look, as if it were a watercolor someone's hand had brushed. "The Monster of Monroe Street. That's what they called your great-great-great-grandpa. He was blood of my blood, and your grandma's, and your mama's."

I brushed the memory away. Aunt Louise was in Florida now and apt to stay there the rest of her life. Foolish to think about her.

If any of these houses were for rent, there were no signs saying so. I would work my way back to Main Street and consult a real estate agent.

Another street sign loomed up. Converse Street. I turned onto it. The street had no sidewalks. Its houses—all of frame, all plainly of early nineteenth- or even eighteenth-century origin—were set more widely apart than the houses on streets closer to the center of town.

I saw a "For Rent" sign.

It stood on a lawn of ankle-high grass and a few even taller weeds. Beyond the lawn rose a two-story house of weathered brown shingles. Its white window frames and shutters needed new paint.

I got out of the Nissan and went up the flagstoned walk. On the tiny porch I rang the bell, waited, rang again. I really hadn't expected anyone to answer the bell. The sign on the lawn did not say "Inquire Within," but instead gave the name and phone number of a real estate agent.

A few feet to the left of the porch was a window. I could see that the shade was more than halfway up. Surely I, as a prospective renter, had a right to peer in that window.

I did, shading my eyes with my hand against the late afternoon sun. Beyond the wide-meshed curtain I could see a small parlor. By either design or accident, the room displayed that most depressing of color combinations, brown and blue. The carpet was light brown, and a sofa and matching overstuffed chair an electric blue. The chair sat beside a fireplace with a wooden mantel, painted green. No doubt it had been many years since the light of a log fire flickered in that room. Now there was a gas heater, set against bricks that walled up the fireplace mouth.

Even without the sign on the lawn, I would have guessed that this house was unoccupied. The room beyond the mesh curtain had an empty, waiting look.

I stopped beside the For Rent sign long enough to make a mental note of the words, "John Mortimer, Real Estate, Main Street." No street number. Evidently this village had never gone in for street numbers. I had seen none on the houses I passed.

In my car I tilted the rearview mirror down and ran a comb through my hair. I recalled how as a child and teenager I had wished my hair was blonde, like my mother's, rather than dark brown like that of the divorced father I scarcely remembered.

But at least my face was less thin than it had been when I left the Morse-Whitlow Clinic several weeks before. Somebody—wasn't it a Mrs. Paley?—has said that there is no such thing as being too rich or too thin. Rich I wouldn't know about. But after I lost Victor—and my desire for food or just about anything else along with him—I proved that there is such a thing as being too thin. I put away my comb and drove back to the center of the village.

After all those quiet residential streets, Main Street was a bit of a shock. Solid rows of cars, parked at an angle, lined the curbs. On the sidewalks, hordes of what I assumed to be vacationers, many of them in shorts and tank tops that revealed expanses of newly sunburned flesh, drifted along, some slurping ice cream cones as they stared into shop windows.

A few yards in front of me a car began to back away from the curb. I pressed my brake. Ignoring the honks of motorists behind me, I held my ground until the car had finished backing out. Then I slid into its place.

I found the Mortimer Real Estate Agency only a few doors from where I had parked. When I walked in, a middle-aged brunette at a desk near the door looked up briefly and then went back to her typing. From a desk near the rear wall, a very tall young man with horn-rimmed glasses got to his feet. "Yes?" I found myself disconcerted by that monosyllable and by the expressionless way his gray eyes stared at me through his glasses. His age, I guessed, was about thirty.

"Mr. Mortimer?"

"No, he's my cousin. I'm Martin Crowley."

He gestured toward a straight chair beside his desk. I sat down, and he folded his six-feet-two-or-three inches back into his swivel chair. He said, "There was something?"

"You have a house for rent on Converse Street."

"Oh, that one. For how long would you want it?"

"Until September."

"Well, if you don't mind there being no garage, you can have it, and at a bargain. One thousand a month. And if you don't

9

think that's a bargain, let me quote you some other prices. People are getting more than that for single rooms with kitchen privileges."

"I know." From fellow employees at the advertising agency I had heard about prices in the Hamptons. "Why is this house so cheap?"

"Well, here it is early July, and the place still isn't rented. People who rent never come back to it the next year. Sometimes they don't even stick it out the first year."

"Why?" I smiled. "Is it haunted?"

"No. Anyway, nobody's ever complained of that, but according to my cousin's records, they've complained about almost everything else."

"What sort of things?"

"Legitimate beefs, some of them. The pipes keep silting up, so that the water runs slow. Once a short circuit in the basement set the place on fire. The damage wasn't extensive, but a lot of video equipment the tenant had brought out from the city was destroyed. Mostly, though, it's been just vague things. People say they find the house depressing. At least twice couples renting that house for the summer have split up before Labor Day." He paused. "You married?"

"No, so I wouldn't have splitting up to worry about. And may I say how much I admire your masterly salesmanship?"

That owlish look became even more pronounced. "Irony, a literary form more favored in England than in America. Do you mean you find my frankness off-putting, Miss—"

"Loring, Gail Loring. I shouldn't think that being *that* frank would help you rent houses. And besides—" I broke off, embarrassed.

"Besides what?"

"It's the way you look at people, or look at me, at least. It's what you might call—"

"Fishy-eyed. I'm sorry. I'm afraid I acquired this stare when I was a teenager, so that I could intimidate people before they intimidated me. I had to wear glasses, and I was six feet tall by the time I was fifteen. In all my class pictures I looked like Ichabod Crane, towering over even the teacher. If they'd played basketball at my high school everything might have been different, but as it was all I had going for me was my stare. Got to be a habit, I guess.

"Anyway," he went on, "even if I was a lousier salesman, I'd still score, what with people pouring out of the city ready to rent anything. Right now I have only three house rentals left, that one on Converse Street and a couple of multibath, Jacuzzi, and swimming pool numbers offered at twenty thousand each for the rest of the summer."

He paused. "You want to look at that house?"

"Yes."

"All right. I'll get my car from the parking lot in back and meet you up there."

A few minutes later we went up the flagstoned walk to the little front porch. He turned a key in the lock, and we stepped inside a short hallway. The air was a bit musty, but not enough so to be unpleasant. Opening the doors and windows to summer sunlight for a few hours would remedy that. To our left was the small parlor I already had seen through the window. To our right was a room of the same proportions, furnished with a studio couch, a few odd straight chairs, and a table piled high with dusty magazines. Its blanked-off fireplace, with a gas heater set against a backing of green metal, was a duplicate of the one across the hall.

"Around 1800," Martin said, "when this house was built, all respectable houses had twin parlors. I don't know why."

Farther back along the hall, beyond the foot of a mahogany-railed staircase, were doors to the kitchen and dining room. The light was growing dim by then, but I could tell that the kitchen appliances, though old, were reasonably clean, and that the dining room table of scarred oak at least appeared serviceable.

We climbed the stairs. There were four bedrooms, with furnishings that ranged from a sagging studio couch to a fairly

11

new-looking double bed in the bedroom above the kitchen. I decided that would be my room, but not just because the bare mattress felt resilient to my testing hand, or because the bathroom, with its claw-footed tub, was right next door. I chose it also because there seemed to be something friendly, even welcoming, about this room, with its fairly new-looking wallpaper—blue nosegays against a silver background—its rag rug faded by many washings, and its kidney-shaped dressing table skirted with blue chintz.

In fact, I was beginning to feel that the whole house had a welcoming quality. Perhaps in time it would manifest some of those shortcomings which had caused it to be dubbed a lemon, but right now I liked the place.

"Well," he was standing slouched in the bedroom doorway, the top of his head almost brushing the top of the doorframe. Despite that curt monosyllable, despite those owlish eyes looking at me with apparent indifference through the fading light, I caught the impression that for some reason he very much wanted me to rent this house. As he stood there, masking his thoughts with that stare, I also felt I knew just how he had looked when he was that six-foot-tall high school freak, the one who might have been the school hero, if only they'd had basketball.

"I'll take it," I said.

"Okay. We'll go back to the office and sign the lease."

Less than half an hour later, with my check lying on his desk, Martin handed me the two-months' lease. "I guess you'll have to stay at a motel for a couple of days," he said, "until the phone and electricity are turned on. I'll attend to that tomorrow. And I'll arrange to have the grass mowed sometime within the next few days."

"Thank you."

"All part of the service. You ought to be able to move in Thursday afternoon at the latest. Oh, something I haven't mentioned. Sheets and blankets don't come with the place."

"I have some in my car. You see, I came out here to share a

12

house with a friend, but it all fell through." With lingering resentment, and more than a light pang of envy, I thought of Beth and Pete, who right at this moment might be boarding the night flight to Paris.

"Then I guess that takes care of everything, except—" He hesitated.

"Except?"

"I was wondering if you would have dinner with me Friday night. You said you'd never been in Hampton Harbor before. I could tell you about it. I've heard some people say it's the most interesting small town in America."

I was about to say, "Is this part of the service too?" But I didn't. I have always been aware of how vulnerable a man is, especially a sensitive man, when he makes his first overture to a woman. Flippancy might make him regret his invitation. And I didn't want him to. I was surprised at how strongly I felt about that. Since Victor, I had not cared a great deal about any man's reaction to me.

"Thank you," I said. "That sounds very nice."

Two

꒜

Near sunset on Thursday I moved into the Converse Street house. I put sheets and blankets on the bed in that back bedroom with the blue-and-silver wallpaper, and then made a brief survey of the rooms on the second floor and the one below. After that I spread the round dining room table with a white cotton cloth I had bought at the Hampton Harbor Variety Store and set a place for myself with the silver I had brought from New York. It was a good thing I'd brought it, too. The silverware in this house consisted of three dull and pitted steak knives, three wooden-handled forks, and four tablespoons. Mysteriously, there were no teaspoons at all.

On the old electric range I cooked the lamb chop and snow peas I had bought at the Main Street supermarket. Then I carried my dinner into the dining room and ate it beneath a droplight with a shade of multicolored glass, which definitely was not by Tiffany, but wasn't too bad all the same.

Midway through my meal I began to feel sleepy. No wonder. Noisy neighbors had kept me awake most of my two nights at the motel. I rinsed and stacked the dishes, and went upstairs to bed.

14

And I dreamed.

A sleeping man was with me in the bed, a man I loathed. My skin seemed to crawl with that loathing. Even though I lay with my back to him, I knew just how he looked, his shape bulky beneath the bed clothes, his mouth red and moist-looking in his bearded face, his eyes slightly open so that some of the white showed. Soon, I knew, he would turn onto his back, and then he would snore.

I lay motionless, eyes open. The room was filled with the mingled glow of moonlight and that of the fire banked in the fireplace. I could see the big cabbage roses on the wallpaper and even the grapevine carving on the tall clothes press leaning against one wall. When an ember flared I even saw the pineapple finial on one of the bed's tall posts.

A whimpering sound came from the room across the hall. I tensed, ready to slip from beneath the bed clothes. If the child began to cry, I would try to soothe her before the man was fully aroused. When awakened during the night he could be furious, which I dreaded, or amorous, which I dreaded even more.

The child apparently had gone back to sleep. I looked for a few minutes more at the mingling of warm fireglow and cool moonlight in the room, and then closed my eyes.

I awoke to see bright sunlight flooding the room. Almost immediately I remembered my dream. Such a strange one, and so vivid. I could still feel the loathing my dreaming self had felt for that black-bearded man.

Had its setting been a dream-altered version of this room? Perhaps. Its proportions had been about the same, and the dream fourposter had been set in about the same spot as this double bed with its maple headboard. But all the other details had been different. Dark wallpaper strewn with pink cabbage roses instead of the silvery paper now glinting in the morning light. A fireplace, glowing with banked coals, where now there was an unbroken wall. That tall wardrobe which, if it had been real, would have fetched a nice price in an antique store. And,

15

of course, the presence of the sleeping man, and of the child in the room across the hall.

Again I marveled at the dream's vividness. As nearly as I could recall, no dream of mine had ever before held such details as a wallpaper's pattern.

I became aware of hunger. I got out of bed, and crossed the hall to the bathroom with its circular showerhead that jutted out over the ancient claw-footed tub. Fifteen minutes later, showered and dressed, I went down to the kitchen and cooked myself a hearty breakfast of scrambled eggs and toast.

After breakfast I spent a few minutes inspecting the backyard with its weed-grown lawn and its small tool shed, empty now of everything except rusted coffee cans and a shovel with the top two-thirds of its handle missing. Then I went out to my car in the driveway and, armed with a map I had bought in a Main Street shop the day before, set out to explore the local beaches. First I went to an appropriately named Long Beach, where a pebble-strewn shoreline curved for about a mile along Noyac Bay. On this windless day the blue, sparkling water was almost as placid as that in a bathtub.

I drove back to Hampton Harbor and then south to Bridgehampton, where giant elms and maples shaded the quiet streets and the old frame houses which, unlike those of Hampton Harbor, sat well apart. I recalled hearing someplace, or perhaps reading, that the early inhabitants of most of the Hamptons, being farmers, had seen no reason to crowd their houses close to one other. But the Harbor's whalemen, whose voyages often lasted a year or more, had tried to see to it that their families had the protection of close neighbors during their absence. Hence all those streets set with houses separated by only a few feet.

Beyond Bridgehampton, I drove through broad potato fields, dotted here and there with large, aggressively modern houses. Even though I had never seen these fields before Wall Street high rollers began to build their awesomely expensive houses here, I felt regret for the unbroken beauty those green fields must once have had. The ocean beaches, though, were

16

still beautiful. Backed by dunes, where wild roses bloomed among the tangles of vines and dune grass, they stretched clean and white to the incoming rollers. Even though the day was fairly cool, beach-goers were plentiful, lying with near-naked, well-oiled bodies glistening in the sun.

I looked at my watch. Ten past twelve. Time to go back to fix my lunch. It was also time for me to wash my hair for my dinner date with Martin Crowley.

Back in Hampton Harbor, I suddenly realized that the street sign I had just passed had said Monroe Street. My heart gave a nervous leap. Perhaps the house I was passing right now, a large house of white clapboard with a pillared porch—

As soon as possible I turned onto another street. That was absurd of me, I told myself. After all, I had decided to spend the summer in this town, despite that story of Great Aunt Louise's which had darkened my late childhood. Anyway, my aunt had been an alcoholic, one of several in my family. Perhaps that story about some monstrously criminal ancestor of ours had been an inebriated fantasy.

Determined not to let anything spoil this sunny day and my anticipation of the evening ahead, I drove to Converse Street, parked my rented car in the driveway, and went into the silent house.

Three

❧

Martin and I dined that night in the garden of a cafe near the Hampton Harbor waterfront. The last of the daylight mingled with the glow of the hurricane lamps on the tables. The cafe's exterior had struck me as extremely modest, but from the first bite I realized that the food rivaled that served by the posh Manhattan restaurants where Victor used to take me. The patrons, though, were not dressed like the ones I had seen at Lutece. Like Martin, many of the men wore summerweight trousers and cotton turtlenecks. The women were equally casual in cotton dresses or pants and tops. I was glad I had chosen a yellow cotton sundress, rather than the navy blue silk suit I had been tempted to wear.

Over our appetizer of artichoke hearts, I asked, "How long have you been in the real estate business?"

"I haven't been. I mean, I'm not now. I'm just holding the fort until my cousin recovers from a bad accident."

"A car crash?"

"Plane. An old Piper Cub he'd been flying for about ten years."

18

"And you can do that? Just leave your own work to take over your cousin's business?"

"Teachers don't work during the summer."

"Teachers!"

He smiled at my astonishment. "I teach English at Ardsmith College."

"I've heard of it. It's part of the state university system, isn't it?"

He nodded. "It's in Rockland County."

"I was an English major in college."

"Who wasn't?"

"You like teaching?"

"I love it."

"And real estate?"

"It's not too bad, not for just the summer. And I like Hampton Harbor. I have ever since I spent summers here as a kid with my aunt and uncle and my cousins. It's such a maverick of a town, so different from the other Hamptons. In fact, it's called the un-Hampton Hampton."

I nodded. That day I'd seen two bicyclists wearing tee shirts with the printed slogan, "Hampton Harbor, the un-Hampton Hampton."

"It's the people who have always made it different," he went on. "The overwhelming majority of farmers and shopkeepers who settled other Hampton villages were of English ancestry. The whaleship owners and captains here in the Harbor were a pretty Waspy lot too. But the crews were polyglot, not just Yankees but Portuguese, Spaniards, American Indians, and even Fiji Islanders. Very early the Harbor developed a split personality. Musicales and champagne and crystal chandeliers in those mansions along Captains' Row— Do you know where that is?

"I think so. It's made up of those beautiful big houses on the residential part of Main Street, isn't it?"

He nodded. "By contrast, the part of town where we are now

19

was wide open. More brothels and grog shops here than in all the rest of eastern Long Island."

"But that was long ago. How about later?"

"The town became even more of a mix. After whaling died out, a watch factory and various small industries tried to replace it. Polish and Italian and Irish immigrants came here to find work. Where once the town was Protestant, it became eighty percent Catholic. Then, about twenty-five years ago, well-off New Yorkers discovered that the Harbor had more fine old houses, many falling into decay, than any other village on eastern Long Island."

"Why more old houses here?"

"Bad times. Ever since whaling collapsed around 1850, the town had been in a depression. There wasn't enough money to tear down those old Colonial and Greek Revival houses and build something up-to-date in their place. The well-heeled New Yorkers bought up the old houses and restored them."

The Chablis Martin had ordered arrived at our table. I watched silently as the waiter went through the ritual of pouring a little wine for Martin to taste, and then filling both our glasses.

When the waiter had gone I said, "And who came after the rich New Yorkers?"

"The intellectuals. Writers, mostly. Each fall they hold something called the Hampton Harbor Symposium. They mull over the state of the world. Then they invite the populace to sit in the high school auditorium while they, seated on the stage, tell us what should be done about AIDS, crime, drugs, and such. The Symposium people tend to be leftish, and most of the natives in this village vote Republican, and so next year everyone expects that there'll be a beef about their using the words Hampton Harbor in the name for their get-together."

I smiled. "Any other new additions to the Harbor mix?"

"Yes. A revival of the sixties sensibility. Rolfing, and est, and all that. There's a shop in town that sells books on everything from astrology to witchcraft. It sells certain paraphernalia too.

I see people of all ages going around the streets with crystal pendants dangling from around their necks. The crystals are to ward off evil vibes, or attract good ones, or something like that."

"And do they? What do you think about it?"

He shrugged. "It's a religion. I suppose, like any other religion, it works for you if you have faith in it. I never could have." He looked at my glass. "Hey! Don't you like your wine? You've scarcely touched it."

"It's delicious." I took a sip. "But I don't drink much."

He smiled. "Why? Afraid of developing a taste for the stuff?"

I returned his smile. "Scarcely that." But of course it was at least partly that.

While I ate the roast chicken with black beans and asparagus the waiter had placed before me, I tried to keep up my end of the conversation. But my thoughts centered around my Great aunt Aunt Louise.

She was my grandmother's elder, unmarried sister, and until my grandmother's death the two women had lived together. After that she moved into the high-ceilinged old apartment where my mother and I lived. I was only seven then, but I can remember the vague depression her presence brought me. Not that I saw much of her. Most of the time she stayed in her room, emerging only to sit at the dinner table, her lined face contrasting with the youthful sheen of her dyed black hair, her words slow and carefully spaced and yet slurred. Sometimes when she was too "sick" to come to the table, my mother sent me into my aunt's room with a dinner tray. I hated to go there. The room always had a mixed smell of cologne and face powder and what I had come to recognize as gin. And almost always, even when outside the midsummer sun still shone brightly, the shades were drawn, so that as I carried the tray through the gloom to the bed I tended to bump into things.

When I complained about Aunt Louise's presence, my mother said, "Would you like for me to take a job? It would mean you would have to go to a day care center in the summer and after school in the winter."

"Oh, no!" I had seen a TV program about day care centers where children were yelled at and shaken and fed terrible food.

"Well, I'd have to take a job if it weren't for what Aunt Louise pays us to live here." Her face set in that bitter expression that always made her look so much older. "Most of that stingy divorce settlement I got from your father is already gone."

My father, a civil engineer, had left us—"ran out on us," my mother phrased it—when I was five. I had not seen him since. He and his new wife lived in a place in South America called Aruba, my mother told me.

Apparently, by the time I was ten my mother decided that I was old enough that she could go to work. Or maybe she became tired of spending her days with her often comatose, yet sometimes numbingly garrulous aunt. (She said things three times. "Your grandmother bought every single record of Frank Sinatra's," she would say to me. "She certainly did. She would buy every record he made.") Anyway, my mother took a job as a saleswoman in a fashionable dress shop over on the East Side.

The next summer, my eleventh, we went as usual to that Jersey shore cottage for a two-week vacation. It was there that Aunt Louise told me about my Hampton Harbor ancestry.

I had come up from the beach about five o'clock, sunburned and sandy in a white tank suit, and found Aunt Louise sitting in the old wicker armchair on the porch. My mother was out buying groceries. I felt surprised to see Aunt Louise because here, just as in the apartment, she spent nearly all her time in her room.

"Sit down," she said. Even though she spaced her words, "sit" sounded like "sid."

I sank onto the top step. I had a feeling, then and later, that she had been waiting for me. Perhaps, brooding over Lord only knew what, she had worked up so much rancor that she had to take it out on someone, and I was not only near but vulnerable.

22

She leaned forward in her chair, a tall, heavy woman in dark purple pants and a beige sweater. "You don't like me, do you?"

I should have protested, of course. But I was so struck by the suddenness as well as the accuracy of the charge that I just sat there, dumb.

"You think I'm just an old drunk, don't you?"

I found my voice. "Oh, no, Aunt Louise."

"Oh, yes, you do. But let me tell you something, girlie. I drink because it's in the blood, yours and mine. Yes, and in your grandmother's too. You know how she died?"

Afraid of what she was about to tell, I said loudly, "She was run over in the street. Outside of her apartment."

"Yes, but do you know why she was run over? She'd been to a cocktail party in the apartment house across the street. She was going back to her own place, blind drunk, and she stepped right in front of this car—"

"That's not true!" I did not remember my grandmother very well, but I liked what I did remember.

"Oh, yes, it is, yes it is. It certainly is."

I heard the Chevrolet my mother had bought two summers before approaching along the road behind the cottage. Evidently the sound had not penetrated my great aunt's self-absorption.

"And I'll tell you something else, girlie. You must think that your mother's a lot better than me, never taking anything but a cocktail now and then."

Sitting rigid, I heard the back door open and close.

"But just you wait. The stuff'll get her too. It's in the blood, I tell you."

I felt a speechless indignation ever so faintly touched with fear.

"Maybe it started, oh, about a hundred and forty years ago, in Hampton Harbor. Yes, just about that long ago. It happened in 1840. Bet you never heard of that town, did you?"

My voice came out thick. "No."

"It's way out on the eastern end of Long Island. A man named

Samuel Fitzwilliam lived there. He was your great-great—Oh, I'm not sure how many greats. But anyway, you're his direct descendant. He owned whaleships, and he lived on Monroe Street. That's why, afterwards, they called him the Monster of Monroe Street. After he did it, I mean. You see, he wasn't just a drinker. He was a killer. That's in your blood, too."

The screen door flew open. My mother stood there, hands on her hips. She said, in a voice shrill with rage, "Gail! Go to your room."

Head lowered, I went into the house and down the hall. In my room I stretched out on the bed. I left my door open, but evidently my mother had closed the front door, because I could not make out the words of the two women on the porch, only the tone of their voices—embattled at first, then quieter. By the time my mother called me for dinner their conflict seemed over. She sat at the table appearing ostentatiously calm and brisk. Aunt Louise appeared ostentatiously meek and silent.

While my mother and I did the dinner dishes, I said. "This man, this Samuel—"

"Just one of those silly family legends." She spoke so promptly that I knew she had been waiting for my questions. "I'm not even sure that we had an ancestor of that name, let alone that he was a—a murderer. Such stories crop up in families. People even take a weird sort of pride in them. Why, I've had two people tell me that they were related to Jack the Ripper, and never mind that even experts can't agree who the Ripper was! And when I was a little girl in Sunday School, a member of the choir told me that she was descended from Dick Turpin, the highwayman. Anyway, I've made Aunt Louise promise not to bring up that story ever again. And you're not to ask her about it."

I began to hang cups on their cupboard hooks. Evidently my mother had not approached the front door in time to hear that ugly prediction about herself and alcohol.

"Will Aunt Louise go on living with us?" For the past couple of hours I had been hoping that my mother had told her that,

24

when we returned to the city, she would have to get an apartment of her own.

"Yes, dear. She would be very unhappy all alone. Besides, her money makes things so much easier for us."

That certainly was true, much as I disliked admitting it. Aunt Louise's money, invested in the long bull market, had grown quite plentiful these past few years. She had increased the amount she paid my mother, with the result being our new furniture, and my mother's Chevrolet.

"We have to make allowances for your Aunt Louise," my mother said. "As for what she told you this afternoon, forget about it. As I said, she's promised never to mention it again."

Aunt Louise kept that promise. Never again did she refer to Samuel Fitzwilliam, or try to convince me that alcohol had caused my grandmother's death, or repeat her prediction that in time "the stuff" would "get" my mother.

Nevertheless, the prediction came true, but not until after I had finished high school and entered Barnard College, whose tuition my mother never could have afforded had it not been for the room-and-board money Aunt Louise paid her.

Three-quarters of the way through my junior year I came home late one afternoon to find my mother and my great aunt in the apartment's dining room. They sat at the oval table with cards spread out in double solitaire formation. Although spring sunlight still shone outside, the room's shades were drawn. Smoke from my aunt's cigarette eddied in the glow of the amber-globed wall lights. A glass of what I knew must be gin and tonic stood beside her ashtray. The fingers of my mother's right hand curled around a shorter glass filled with brown liquid—bourbon and plain water, I later learned.

She smiled at me as if this were any ordinary afternoon. "Hello, baby. How was school?"

"Fine."

"You mind fixing your own dinner and eating it in the breakfast nook? There's ham and tomatoes and potato salad in the fridge. I don't feel like cooking tonight, or even eating."

Most days after that they drank together, sometimes in the dining room, sometimes in Aunt Louise's room, but always with the shades drawn. (I often thought of something I had read somewhere: The alcoholic's favorite hours are the dark ones.) I suppose some might have found certain comic aspects in a middle-aged woman and an elderly one boozing together day after day behind drawn shades. But I loved my mother too much to find it in the least funny.

I don't know why my mother suddenly turned to liquor. Maybe it was because of something in her life I did not know about. Certainly I had gathered that there was a man, the brother of the dress shop's owner, whom she would have liked to pay attention to her. Maybe he had turned to someone else, thus causing her to reach for the bottle. Or perhaps—sickening thought—Aunt Louise was right about drinkers being afflicted with some sort of curse, something "in the blood." Perhaps she had held out against a thirst for years. Now that I was almost through college, she felt that she could give in to it.

I finished my days at Barnard. My mother and Aunt Louise— my mother cold sober, my aunt almost so—attended my graduation. A week after that I took a job with the Horton and Jedlow advertising agency.

And two weeks after that my mother, driving home after the Brownsville wedding of her boss's daughter, hurtled her second-hand Buick off the parkway and into a tree trunk. She died—instantly, they told me—of a broken neck. I did not have to wait for the coroner's report to know that she must have been drunk.

Numb with grief, I rode with Aunt Louise in the funeral home limo to a cemetery in Queens. In incongruously bright midsummer sunlight I stood beside the open grave while the minister of the Episcopalian church we had almost never attended read the burial service.

As soon as we had returned to the apartment I said, "Aunt Louise, I have to talk to you."

She faced me, alarm and pugnacity gathering in her clumsily made-up dark eyes. "Well?"

"You've always said you envied your friends who have condominiums in Florida. I want you to go there now, or at least somewhere. I want to sell this big old apartment and move into a small one, by myself."

"You want me to live in Florida?" she cried. "Why, down there it's so hot five months of the year that—"

"Not in northern Florida."

"Your mother lying in her grave only two hours, and already you're trying to throw me into the street!"

"You wouldn't have to stay in the street, not with your money. Besides, I wouldn't expect you to leave tomorrow. But soon, just as soon as possible."

"Your mother wouldn't like your doing this!"

"I know. But I have to do it. I can't go on living with you. I shouldn't think you would want to live with me, now that Mother is gone. You've never liked me, have you?"

She didn't answer that but said, "You're a cold, wicked girl. You don't feel any grief, any respect for your mother's memory."

She was wrong. I felt a paralyzing grief. I wanted to get free of my aunt before that numbness wore off. In the weeks ahead, I felt, I would not be able to cope with both my grief and her unwelcome presence.

For three weeks she stayed on in the apartment, giving one excuse after another—a sinus attack, business with her broker—for not leaving. Then, all of a sudden, she was gone. I heard her on the phone one Saturday morning, talking to a friend in Tampa. That evening she was on her way to Kennedy and a Florida-bound plane.

By that time I had arranged to sell my mother's apartment and to sub-lease a smaller one in the same building. I would have preferred to live in another building and even another part of town. But unless you were rich, available apartments were rare. I had some of my mother's furniture moved down to my

27

apartment, and put the rest in storage, along with a few pieces
that had belonged to my great aunt.

Now Martin said, across the little restaurant table, "How about
dessert? They make a tasty blueberry tart here."

Twenty minutes later we emerged into the glow of the full
moon. It was so bright that I could read the words, *Wave
Dancer,* on the hull of a yacht anchored in the marina across
the road.

"I was going to suggest we listen to music one place or
another," he said, "but it seems to me that this moonlight is too
good to waste."

"I agree."

We drove toward Bridgehampton and then turned off onto
a series of winding back roads, almost deserted at this hour.
That eerily bright radiance silvered the roads, the occasional
ponds we passed, and the roofs of the widely scattered houses.
No aggressively modern architecture here. Even the structures
Martin identified as new had a nineteenth-century farmhouse
look.

Once he switched off the headlights. We moved slowly along
a road lit only by the moon. Martin said, "Now we can imagine
what it must have been like to ride along here in a horse-drawn
buggy a hundred years ago."

"Very nice, as long as some lurking cop doesn't catch you."

"Right," he said, and switched on the lights.

The hands of the dashboard clock pointed to almost eleven-
thirty. "I feel sleepy," I said. "Maybe it's because I spent the
whole day in the open air."

We turned back to Hampton Harbor and drove along its
tangle of narrow, curving streets, where only a few windows
were still lit, to my rented house on Converse Street. When we
had stopped at the curb, Martin turned to me. "Too sleepy to
ask me in for coffee?"

"I'm afraid so." I knew that more than coffee would be
involved.

28

He understood. "Is it too soon? Or is it that I just don't appeal to you?"

"It's not that," I said, swiftly and truthfully. I liked nearly everything about him, his gangling height, and his wry but good-humored observations about this village and its people, and even that owlish stare of his.

He said, "Then I guess my next line should be, who was he?"

As I looked at him, uncomprehending, he said, "Then you say, 'What do you mean?' And I say, 'The man who did this to you.' " He paused. "Or wasn't there any special man?"

"There was." Instantly I regretted telling him that. It might lead to more questions. And so far I'd talked in detail about Victor only with my woman shrink at the clinic.

He asked no more questions, though. He waited for a few seconds and then said, smiling, "Maybe you'll tell me about it some day."

We went up the flagstone walk. I could smell the fragrance of grass mowed only that afternoon. On the front porch he took the key from my hand and turned it in the lock. I liked that, too. None of my other dates had unlocked my door for me.

He said, swinging the door wide and then handing me the key, "Weekends are the busiest time in the real estate business. But if you like, we could have dinner Monday night."

Better not, I thought, and heard myself say, "I'd like that."

He kissed me lightly, said goodnight, and went down the walk. Inside the house I switched on the light in the little hall. I heard his car start up and drive away.

*F*our

❧

I looked at the stairs leading upward. The memory of that dream came to me. Firelight mingling with the light of an almost full moon. Cabbage roses on dark wallpaper. The unseen bulk of the man lying beside me in the bed.

Suddenly I found myself reluctant to go upstairs just yet. Turning, I went through the front door and out into the flood of blue-white radiance. With the thought of that dream still clinging to me, I went around the house and, walking over the fragrant grass, moved toward the back yard.

For some reason I could not have defined, I halted near the rear corner of the house and looked at its brown shingle wall. I saw something I had not noticed in broad daylight. Just beyond the kitchen window an area of larger and just-a-shade-darker shingles rose to the eaves. It looked as if there had been a chimney there at one time, serving a fireplace in the kitchen and one in the bedroom directly above. A fireplace that must have been located just about where the one in my dream had been—

So what, I told myself. As we drove along those deserted

30

back roads, Martin had mentioned that back in the last century even modest houses had had several fireplaces. In time their owners, for convenience's sake or in an eagerness to be up-to-date, had installed furnaces and blanked off fireplaces indoors. Outdoors they had ripped away chimneys and then covered up the wounds with new shingles or clapboards, as the case might be.

I went around the house and sat down on the back step. Looking at the about-to-collapse tool shed, I tried to think of nothing except what I would do the next day. First of all I'd lay in more groceries. Then I'd look at the art galleries in the village. In the afternoon I'd drive over to the ocean for a swim.

At last I was beginning to feel sleepy again. Because I'd locked the kitchen entrance before leaving the house that evening, I walked around to the front of the house and through its open door.

I had thought—half expectantly, half uneasily—that I might dream again of that room with the cabbage rose wallpaper. I did not. Instead, when I awoke after eight hours of unbroken sleep, I could recall only a remnant of an ordinary, although worrisome, dream about guests arriving at my New York apartment for a party I had forgotten I was to give.

Thin clouds had swept in during the night, so that the sunlight filtering through them was pale. No matter. I would still enjoy my gallery-going and my swimming. I showered in the claw-footed tub, dressed, and went downstairs. The entrance to the kitchen from the hall was furnished with a louvered swinging door, one which looked as if it had been installed in the last ten years or so.

I pushed the door open.

A creaking sound. At the wooden sink, Sara's skinny black arm was working the pump handle up and down, up and down. The air held a smell of burning food.

"Sara!" I cried. "The griddle cakes!"

She turned, thin as a wisp in her voluminous gray calico

31

dress, aging face aghast in its frame of white turban. "Oh, Miz Martha! I clean forgot."

She scuttled over to the fireplace and knelt. " 'Twere that pesky pump," she grumbled. "A body has to work it and work it—"

A roaring in my ears drowned out her words. And I could not see very well. A gathering mist threatened to blot out the fire's glow and the weak sunlight coming through the window. I reached out, grasped the back of a wooden chair, and managed to lower myself onto its seat.

The mist dissolved. So did the whole hallucination. The chair on which I sat was not a wooden ladderback, but one made of steel tubing with a plastic seat. A tall matching stool stood beside the porcelain sink, with its two faucets. Across the room, where my sick mind had conjured up a fireplace with an old black woman kneeling in front of it, stood the electric range on which I had cooked the previous day.

My stomach gathered itself into a knot. I was aware of sweat springing out on my forehead and upper lip. So Dr. Helen Vorney, that shrink at the clinic, had been wrong about me. I was still sick, and probably always would be.

I sat there, too despairing even to stir from the chair.

*F*ive

In a way, it was because of Victor that I landed in the Morse-Whitlow Clinic.

My mother had been dead less than six months when Victor Manning joined the advertising firm where I worked. Like me, he was given the title of junior copy writer. Through coffee break gossip his first day on the job, I learned that he didn't need it. His father was CEO of Burnham Investments, a major Wall Street firm. What was more, a grandmother had left him a substantial inheritance. If he had been a European, chances are good that he would never have taken a job. Instead he would have passed his time skiing in the Alps and acquiring a tan aboard boats of varying tonnage in the Mediterranean. But American young men, no matter how rich, are expected to work at something, even if it's only politics.

Besides wealth, he had good looks. He looked like a more masculine version of one of those men in the Armani ads. The same thick hair, dark in his case. The same classic features, including a well cut mouth with a full lower lip. When he smiled, his forehead wrinkled. For some reason, I found that quizzically wrinkling forehead one of the most attractive things about him.

When, during his first week on the job, he asked me to have lunch with him, I was too astonished even to feel flattered. Why me? I was passably attractive, but I had no illusions about being more than that. Maybe I reminded him of a favorite cousin. Or maybe he had the mistaken notion that as a copy writer I possessed some special expertise I could pass on to him.

The next week he twice took me to dinner. I still had not been able to discern any reason for his attentiveness. When I confided my puzzlement to my friend Beth, who was still working at the agency, she said, "Oh, for heaven's sake, Gail. Who knows what anybody sees in anybody? What does it matter? Why don't you say to yourself, 'This simply terrific guy has a yen for me, so I'm going to relax and enjoy it.'?"

I was ready to follow that advice. In fact, by that time I was thoroughly in love.

A month later I told him about my mother and great aunt drinking together in shade-dimmed rooms. And I told him of that earlier afternoon when, on the beach cottage porch, Aunt Louise had weighted my eleven-year-old spirit with her talk of my dark legacy.

"Why, the drunken old bitch!" Victor said. Then, after a moment, he chuckled. "Well, she certainly missed on one count. If alcoholism is a curse in your family it missed you. I've seen you make a glass of wine last through a whole cocktail party." Again he paused and then asked, "But what about this ancestor who lived in Hampton Harbor way back when?"

"My mother said it was just a story that's been handed down in the family. I've told you all I know."

I would not have revealed to him the dark aspects of my growing up if by then we had not become lovers, sometimes spending most of the weekend in my apartment, more often in his East Fifty-seventh Street condo, a small place handsomely furnished by the decorator from whom Victor had bought the apartment. Deeply in love, I felt he had the right to know everything about me.

Neither of us had actually said it out loud, but I had little doubt that we would eventually get married. Often he spoke of our joint future. "Next summer let's go to Italy."

"Oh, lovely!"

"Let's drive from the heel of the boot up the Adriatic coast. It's still comparatively untouched. When I was there ten years ago with my parents, we saw Crusaders' castles, some in ruins, others at least partially restored. One was for sale. It was a tall round tower. There were six floors, each consisting of just one room with a connecting stone staircase. Maybe we could buy such a place. It would be a damn good investment. Maybe, if things work out right, we could live there at least part of the year. How would you like being the chatelaine of a thirteenth-century round tower?"

"It sounds wonderful." I think I would have said the same thing if he had proposed that we live part of the year in an igloo near the North Pole.

I learned what people mean when they speak of another person becoming "one's whole life." All the things I used to enjoy—gallery-going, leisurely Saturday lunches with Beth, jogging around the Central Park reservoir—all became dull in comparison with the hours I sat with Victor in a restaurant, aware of the envious glances of other women, or lay beside him in bed, with his perpetually tanned hands caressing my body. I had always liked my job. It had been fun, trying to find just the right phrase to put a client's tennis racquet, say, ahead of the competition. But if Victor for any reason had asked me to quit my job, I would not have hesitated a moment.

A reactionary attitude? Of course. But you see, I felt that Victor had created me. Before I knew him I had been a rather subdued person. Victor, I was convinced, had turned me into a Gail Loring who otherwise would not have existed, a self-confident, amusing, even beautiful young woman. Surely I

35

must be all those things. Otherwise I would not still have Victor.

The first warning signs appeared about six months after our affair began. I ignored them. It was easy to do so. I just assumed he was telling the truth when he said that he had to break our dinner date in order to entertain an elderly Boston couple, cousins of his mother, or that he couldn't go with me to the theater because he was taking work home from the office, or that he had to spend the weekend with his parents at their Westchester home because they were celebrating their thirty-fifth wedding anniversary. Why shouldn't I have believed him? After all, almost in the same breath, he told me that his parents wanted him to bring me home for the weekend "soon."

When he did finally tell me the truth, it was on a Sunday night as we lay in bed. My bed. For several weeks now, using one excuse or another, he had avoided taking me to his apartment.

As I lay there, warm and relaxed in the afterglow of our love-making, he said, "I've got something to tell you."

People who have good news to impart say, "Guess what?" I've-got-something-to-tell-you almost always presages bad news. But in my warm bliss, I took no warning.

The bedroom door stood partly open, admitting a fan of light from the living room lamps. I turned my head on the pillow to look at him. He lay on his back, hands clasped behind his head. Only the seriousness of his tone prevented me from drawing my forefinger along that classic profile from forehead to chin, as I often did. "What is it, darling?"

"I'm quitting my job. I'm going to work for Dad's firm."

His father's firm. I felt dismay. With him working down on Wall Street, we probably would not be lunching together as often as before. "But why, darling?"

"I wouldn't do it if I were really crazy about the advertising business, but I'm not. Besides, Dad's not well, and I know how much he has always wanted me to join the family business."

36

His voice trailed off. I asked, "When did you decide to do this?"

"I've been thinking about it for about six weeks."

"Why didn't you tell me so?"

"It's—it's hard to talk about something like this. You see, there's more to it."

For the first time, I felt a premonition. "More to it?"

"I'm going to get married. The announcement will be in the *Times* next Sunday."

I couldn't believe I had heard him correctly. A man, having just made love to his adoring girl for perhaps the hundredth time, just does not tell her while still lying in bed beside her that he is going to marry someone else.

"I'm afraid I didn't hear—"

He turned his head to look at me. "Gail, I'm sorry. I'm so sorry."

So I had heard correctly. I said, through numb lips, "Who is she?"

"Her name is Cecily, and she's a distant cousin of my father's. In fact, her last name is the same as mine and his."

I forced the words out. "How can you marry her when you love me?"

He raised himself on one elbow and looked down at me, tanned shoulders and chest gleaming faintly in the light from the living room. "I did love you, Gail. I think I still do. But I have to be realistic. There is more to life than what you and I have had together. There's more than we've even discussed. Children, for instance. I want children."

Again I managed to move my lips. "Why couldn't they be my children?"

"Oh, Gail, Gail! You must know the answer to that. There's—alcoholism in your family. A way back, perhaps something much worse. Maybe you would be willing to take a chance. I'm not. I *can't.*"

I knew that later on I would shrink from the memory of having argued with him, pleaded with him, but right then I couldn't help myself. "You yourself said that I showed no sign of—"

"I know. And you don't, right now. But perhaps later on—"

So much for "sharing everything" with the man you loved. If I had not done so, would we have been engaged, even married, by now? Perhaps. On the other hand, perhaps he had known all along that he would not marry a little nobody from West Eighty-seventh Street.

"When did you ask her to marry you?"

"About six weeks ago. Again and again I've wanted to tell you, but I just couldn't bring myself—"

He went on talking about how painful these past weeks had been for him. Only half listening, I thought, so that's why lately he's managed it that we come here to make love. It would not have done for his fiancée to drop in on him at his apartment and find me there.

There is a movie classic, *Lost Horizon*. At its end, a woman who has lived all her life in the valley called Shangri-la leaves it for the world outside. Once away from the valley's youth-preserving atmosphere, she swiftly withers. In a last, shocking close-up, she appears to be her true age, which is more than a century old.

I felt like that woman now. Oh, not that I felt old. On the contrary, I had a weary sense of all the years stretching ahead of me. But I did feel stripped of all those qualities with which Victor's love had made me feel endowed—charm, wit, physical attractiveness.

He was saying something about how tough it was to belong to a family which expected certain things of you, especially when it came to choosing a wife. I cut through his words.

"Did you know when you came here tonight that you were going to tell me this?"

"Yes." His handsome face looked wretched. "I realized I couldn't put it off any longer."

"Then why did you make love to me tonight?"

38

"Because I couldn't help myself. You see, in spite of what I'm going to do, what I have to do, I still need you——"

I thought of things to say. Scathing, obscene things. Afterwards I was glad I hadn't said them.

"Gail——" He reached his hand toward me.

"Don't touch me." My voice was thick. I turned over in bed and clutched my pillow with both hands. "Don't ever touch me again."

I lay with my eyes closed. For what seemed a long time there was no sound. Then I was aware of him getting out of bed, gathering up his clothes from a chair, going into the living room. After a while I heard the apartment's front door open and close.

It took me almost three months after that to land in the Morse-Whitlow Clinic.

At first I thought I could hack it, despite the feeling that, emotionally speaking, my spinal cord had been severed. True, I had only a few hours of broken sleep each night. True, I kept losing weight, despite my efforts to force food down a permanently constricted throat. But I was not going to fade away, like some maiden in a nineteenth-century poem, just because my lover had turned to someone else. It was the reason he had given for his decision that devastated me. If he had told me just that he had fallen in love with this Cecily, I still would have suffered, but in time I might have been able to cope with the pain. The reasons he had given me, though, stripped me of self-esteem, and therefore of hope.

A few days before Christmas I sat in my cubbyhole office, trying to concentrate on my copy for a perfume ad. My door opened and my boss, Howard Ames, a middle-aged, overweight man whose easy smiles hid the temperament of a Marine drill instructor, lay a typed page on my desk. "This shampoo copy just won't do, Gail. Where's the zing you put into your last ad for this client?"

It was far from his sternest criticism of my work. When I first joined the agency, he had been merciless. His most scathing comments had left me only briefly depressed. Now, though, I lowered my head onto my crossed arms, and burst into tears.

Hand on my shoulder, Howard said, "Now, now," in a tone both embarrassed and alarmed. I went on crying. I had wept very little since that last night with Victor. Now my tears poured forth in a flood.

And it seemed to be an endless flood. Soon I was aware that others had come into the office, including my recently married friend Beth. "Gail!" she said. "Stop that, stop it."

I went on crying. "I'd better take her home," I heard her say.

I wept in the descending elevator, and in the cab that carried us through the park to my apartment. With Beth holding onto my arm, I stumbled into the bedroom. Still crying, I fell face down onto the bed I had so often shared with Victor.

Sometime later I was aware of her talking on the living room phone. Still later, when the room had begun to fill with shadows, Dr. Korngold walked in carrying a black bag. Although he had been our family doctor as long as I can remember, I had not seen him for more than a year. I go to doctors as little as possible.

He asked me what was wrong. When I didn't answer, just shook my head, he went into the bathroom for a moment and then came back. "Here, take this."

I took the glass of water and the pill he held out to me. He went into the living room. I heard his voice and Beth's, both pitched low. After a while he came back into the bedroom. I had stopped crying by then.

"Your friend is going to spend the night here and tomorrow too."

Thanks to the pill, I suppose, I slept that night, leaden, dreamless sleep. When I awoke, though, it was with no will whatsoever to get out of bed. I wanted to please Beth by getting up, or at least by eating the breakfast she brought me, but I couldn't manage it.

Dr. Korngold telephoned me in the afternoon. From the questions he asked—when had my "engagement" been broken, how many pounds had I lost since then, how severe had my "sleep disturbances" been—I knew that Beth had briefed him thoroughly.

At last he said, "This has all the earmarks of clinical depression. I'm going to check you into the Morse-Whitlow Clinic. Now that doesn't mean I think you're crazy," he added swiftly. "But a full-fledged depression can be almost as disabling as a psychosis."

I managed to say, "I can't afford—"

"Your medical insurance ought to pay for most of it. Besides, I told your friend last night that I might recommend the clinic, and this morning she phoned your office." Vaguely I remembered hearing Beth on the phone. "Your employers say that they'll help pay for your hospitalization. They must value your services, probably far more than you realize."

Did they? I found it didn't matter to me whether they did or not.

The clinic, over on the East River, seemed a cheerful place. The rooms were decorated in bright colors. The doctors and nurses almost always smiled. Only the patients were sad. Not one of us on that all-woman floor was violent. None believed herself to be Garbo or Joan of Arc. We were just women who had found ourselves unable to cope. Unable to cope with a man, or the loss of a man. Unable to cope with motherhood, or a career, or a craving for drugs.

I took my medication each day and exercised in the rec room to a disco beat. Each afternoon I spent a half hour to an hour, depending upon how strong my nerves were that day, with the woman psychiatrist assigned to me. She was a pretty, rather plump blonde in her forties, and her name was Helen Vorney.

Over and over again she said, using one phraseology or another, "Authorities disagree about whether a tendency to alcoholism can be inherited. Whether it can or not, you obviously haven't inherited it. Otherwise you would have started hitting the bottle after Victor threw you over."

As for Victor himself, she said, "I don't care if he is as good looking as young John Kennedy or as rich as Donald Trump. A decent man would have taken responsibility for breaking with you. He wouldn't have blamed your family history, something you couldn't help. He was a no-good heel"—only she used an earthier term—"and you're lucky to be rid of him."

Easy enough for her to talk. She had never lain in Victor's arms.

In late April the clinic, evidently believing that they had patched me together well enough to last a while, discharged me. "But remember you can turn to us at any time," Dr. Vorney said. "Now your leave of absence from your job lasts until September. Enjoy those months. Go to the movies or a play every day, if you want. Go to the Metropolitan Museum." She grinned. "I hear that very superior singles go there to pick up each other among the Titians and Rembrandts. Once or twice I've thought of trying my luck there myself."

I went back to my apartment and tried to follow Dr. Vorney's advice, all except that part about the Metropolitan Museum. I didn't want to meet a new man, however superior. I wasn't ready to take the emotional risk. I might never be.

Then, that steaming afternoon last week, a tearful Beth had telephoned and lured me to, of all towns, Hampton Harbor.

Now I sat in that quite ordinary kitchen where, only moments ago, my sick mind had conjured up a wooden sink, and a wooden-handled pump, and a fireplace with an elderly black woman—a slave?—kneeling in front of it. The hallucination had been so vivid that even now I felt I could detect the odor of scorched griddle cakes.

Perhaps Dr. Vorney was correct in believing I was not an incipient alcoholic. But she was wrong in dismissing the idea of an even graver infirmity.

What had I come into this room for? Oh, yes. I'd been hungry. I wasn't hungry now.

I left the kitchen, ran up the stairs, picked up my handbag from the dressing table in the room I had chosen as a bedroom. Downstairs, I didn't even bother to lock the front door behind me. I got into my car and drove toward the ocean.

Six

Halfway to Bridgehampton I began to see ribbons of mist hovering above the asphalt road. Later I learned that this was a frequent phenomenon. The harbor would remain sunny while ocean mist swept in to shroud Bridgehampton and its surrounding fields.

By the time I reached Bridgehampton's wide streets the fog was so thick that I turned on my headlights and slowed to a crawl. Approaching cars, their headlights on, appeared first just as twin circles of pale light, then as dim shapes creeping past me. I drove along roads through level fields, turned onto one that led behind the beach dunes, then onto a narrow, barely visible track that led to the beach.

As nearly as I could tell in this thick smother, mine was the only car there. This was no day for beach going. I switched off my engine and sat there, listening to the thump-and-seethe of incoming breakers a few yards away through the fog.

It was my need to think that had driven me from the house. It was not fear, at least not fear of the house itself. Oddly, the house still seemed to me a friendly place. Nor was there anything frightening in the hallucination that had followed my opening the kitchen door. It had seemed so real, so almost everyday. The black woman working the pump handle, myself sniffing the air with its smell of burned food—

Myself.

Now I did feel a cold ripple down my spine. The hallucination had not been a scene playing itself out before my eyes. I had been a part of it. Just as clearly as I could remember getting dressed in jeans and a blue tee shirt that morning, I could recall stepping into the kitchen in my brown muslin dress, sniffing the air, realizing with annoyance that Sara always seemed to be burning things lately—

It was as if I had an alter-ego, a woman who wore the voluminous dresses of the last century and had an absent-minded domestic named Sara.

And a husband?

I thought of the bedroom where the glow of a banked fire had mingled with moonlight. I thought of the bulky, dark-bearded man beside me in the bed, a man I could visualize even though my back was turned to him. I thought of the child, whimpering in its sleep, beyond the open door of the room across the hall.

I had considered it just a dream, remarkable in its vividness, but otherwise like any other dream. Now, though, it seemed to me the sort of waking dream we call a hallucination, like the one I had experienced in the kitchen.

And if not that, what had it been? What was happening to me?

Fear really gripped me then, a bewildered fear that sped my heart beats and turned my hands cold. What should I do? Try to find out where Dr. Vorney was staying on Cape Cod and telephone her there? No, I really wouldn't want her to return to Manhattan on my account even if she were willing to, which was not too likely. In self protection, psychiatrists and psycho-analysts had to harden themselves against patients who were apt to go into a panic as soon as their doctor left town. Should

I go back to my apartment, then, and consult some other psychiatrist at the clinic? I found I did not want to do that either.

Then what did I want to do? Go on staying in that house?

With jarring abruptness, I realized that the answer was yes.

From the moment I went up the flagstoned walk and peered through a window curtain in that ordinary-looking living room, the house had seemed to draw me into it, almost as if, in some way, I belonged there, almost as if it recognized me.

But even a believer in supernatural phenomena would find that idea absurd. I thought, with an inward shudder, now if it had been a house on Monroe Street— But it was not. Until I saw its For Rent sign, I'd not had the slightest connection with that house or its past in any way, at least none that I knew of.

If I left Hampton Harbor and returned to Manhattan and whatever aid and comfort the clinic doctors might give me, I would never know the truth. For the rest of my life I would wonder whether what I had experienced in that house was the product of a sick mind, or had in some way a reality of its own.

The fog was beginning to lift, almost like a curtain in the theater. Even though thick mist still hovered above the beach, I could see beneath it to a stretch of sand, and beyond it white breakers rushing shoreward over gray water.

I started the engine, backed, turned, and headed toward Hampton Harbor.

Seven

❧

As I turned into my driveway, I saw a woman on the neighboring lawn. With a pair of clippers, she was trimming stray shoots from the privet hedge that separated my rented property from the house next door, a saltbox of brown shingles. When I emerged from the car she said, "Morning." She was a small woman with gray hair cut in a Dutch bob, wearing bright red pants and a pink cotton shirt.

"Hello," I said.

"I'm Emma Blaisdell."

"Gail Loring."

She cocked her head to one side. "Rented the house for the rest of the summer?"

"That's right, until Labor Day."

"All by yourself?"

I nodded.

"New York girl?"

"Yes."

"You some kind of artist or writer or something?"

"No. I sketch a little, but I never even thought of trying to sell my pictures. What made you think I might be—"

"Stands to reason, don't it? Folks with regular jobs can't walk away from them for weeks at a time."

Something in the regard of her bright blue eyes reminded me that besides artistic callings there were others which might enable a young woman to get by without visible means of support. I had best explain myself.

"I've taken a leave of absence from my job, Mrs. Blaisdell."

"Miss. Miss Blaisdell. As I always say, I've got a parrot that swears and a chimney that smokes and a cat that stays out all night, so what do I need with a husband?"

I laughed politely at the ancient wheeze.

She said, "Leave of absence? You one of these new women soldiers?"

"No. I'm in advertising." From inside my house came the sound of the telephone, freeing me from the inquisition. I said, "There's my phone. Nice to have met you, Miss Blaisdell."

In the hurry of my departure from the house I had not locked the front door. Thus I was able to reach the phone on the hall table before it had completed its fifth ring.

Martin said, "Didn't wake you up, did I?"

"Oh, no. I've been awake for hours."

"I was wondering if you'd like to have dinner with me tomorrow."

I hesitated for a moment or two and then said, "That would be great."

It wasn't just that I liked him and found him physically attractive, although I did. I even found his account of his high school years, when he had towered awkwardly over even his teachers, somehow touching and endearing. But I also felt that he offered my best chance of finding out more about this house.

I would not tell him what I had experienced here, though. Nor would I tell him about the alcoholic haze in which the women of my family had lived, nor about a remote male ancestor whose contemporaries had called him a monster. One thing my experience with Victor had taught me: where a man is

48

concerned, keep your own counsel. Otherwise he may turn and rend you someday with what you've told him.

Martin said, "Pick you up at eight o'clock?"

"Eight sounds fine."

The rest of that day and all the next, each time I opened the door into a room I kept half hoping, half fearing that I would find myself back in a world of floor-sweeping dresses and kitchen fireplaces. I did not. The kitchen's enamel stove and discolored porcelain sink remained in place. The other rooms were still decorated in what you might call Summer Rental Moderne, including old but undistinguished overstuffed furniture and new and undistinguished steel tubing and plastic.

By the time Martin arrived to take me to dinner, the weather had turned overcast and damp. It was no night for moonlight driving, and so after dinner at a Main Street restaurant we started walking toward a club located on the wharf jutting several hundred yards into the harbor. Near the foot of Main Street I stopped, my attention caught by a yellowed photograph in a plate glass window. It showed two pairs of mules drawing a platform mounted on rollers down a tree-lined street. On the platform stood a saltbox cottage.

I said, "Look at that!"

"A house moving. That was a favorite activity here in the Harbor back in the last century. Some houses were moved three or four times."

My nerves tightened. A house moving. That was something that had not occurred to me. I looked at the wooden sign above the plate glass window. It said, in gilt letters, *Hampton Harbor Advocate, Est. 1857.*

Martin said, "It's the oldest of our two newspapers."

"Two newspapers! In a town this size?"

"I know." We turned and walked on down the street. "I told you Hampton Harbor is a quirky town. Some would say there's only about enough news to fill four pages. But some time back the *Advocate* expanded to twenty pages. At the same time a rival paper, the *Messenger,* started up. All this extra newsprint to dispose of, just when the local dump has closed down. Incidentally, what do you plan to do about your trash?"

"I hadn't considered the question." All the time he spoke I had been thinking about that yellowed photograph.

"I would advise calling a carter. That is, unless you enjoy hauling trash about the countryside."

"All right. I'll call someone. Martin, the house I'm in. Has it always been where it is now?"

"Good lord! I suppose so. What makes you think it might not have been?"

I said, after a moment, "It's larger than the houses near it. And when I saw that photograph of a house being moved—"

"Well, as far as I know, that house you've rented was built right where it is now. But I suppose you could find out for sure."

The first person to ask, I thought, would be my neighbor, Miss Blaisdell.

We had reached the wharf. The club did not open until eleven, and yet already a line of people stretched from the club entrance back along a row of boutiques almost to the street.

We joined the line. I thought of how Martin had mentioned that early in the last century Hampton Harbor had handled more tonnage than the port of New York. I thought of how the wharf must have looked on a night like this 150 years in the past, lined by ships—sleek schooners and broad, clumsy whalers—with their bare masts swaying against the overcast sky. I thought of the crews lining the rails to look down at the wharf. Because of old illustrations I knew how they would have been dressed, the ordinary seamen in homespun trousers and jerseys, the officers in broadcloth trousers and coats—the tails cut short lest, when they took to the small boats in pursuit of a whale, their clothing become entangled in the lines. Yes, I knew more or less how they had looked. But what would they have made of this wharf now, with its lighted shop windows and its long line of tanned, chattering young people? Especially what would they have made of the two girls who stood in front

50

of us? They wore tank tops and short, tight skirts. And it was obvious from their talk that they were both stockbrokers associated with a famous firm.

I had a sense of time as a broad river, with currents that moved at varying speeds. This weather-beaten wharf and the old town behind it belonged to a slow current, so slow that some of the streets probably looked about the same as they had generations ago. People flowed past it and through it at a much faster clip—colonists in knee breeches giving way to Jacksonians in stovepipe hats and then to prosperous whalers and then to impassioned abolitionists and then, finally, to stockbrokers in miniskirts. Before its own slow-moving current carried the old wharf to oblivion, what other sorts of people might walk along it? Tour groups of Tibetan monks? Vacationing extraterrestrials?

Evidently the club's doors had opened, because the line began to move. Inside, we sat at a balcony table Martin had reserved. From there we had a good view of the stage. When we chose, we could descend stairs to the dance floor.

For a while the big room was filled with that roaring waterfall sound, made up of hundreds of voices talking, laughing, sometimes shouting. Then the roar gave way to an expectant hush. The band had come on stage. It consisted of four musicians, all skeletally thin and with traditionally long hair. The lights along the walls went low, strobe lights criss-crossed the dimness, and the band's guitarist struck a chord.

The music was good, soft reggae. We danced now and then, but spent most of the time looking from our table at the crowd below. We left the club soon after one o'clock. Once we were well away from the wharf area, where teenagers too young to enter the club clutched beer cans and pretended to be much drunker than they were, the village was almost as quiet as it must have been late at night a century ago. The old houses showed only an occasional lit window, and the streets were almost empty of cars.

When we stopped before my rented house I feared that he

would again suggest that he come in for "coffee." Instead he said, smiling at me through the refracted light from the dashboard, "I'll call you very soon. Okay?"

"Of course." So perverse is human nature—or at least my nature—that I felt disconcerted that he had *not* proposed coming in. Had he decided that he didn't want to go to bed with me after all?

But when he had walked with me up to the little porch, and unlocked the door, and handed back the key, he kissed me. His kiss was ardent enough that I no longer feared he found me undesirable. He was just waiting for some signal from me before making another try.

I went inside. In the little entrance hall I stood still for a moment, hearing his car drive away, and looking at the stairs. Again I wondered if another dream, or hallucination, or whatever it had been, would change the wallpaper and fill the bedroom with dim fireglow.

I lay awake for quite a while that night, but when I finally dropped off my sleep was sound. When I awoke to find sunlight flooding through the window, I could remember no dreams at all.

*E*ight

Still in my blue cotton nightgown, I went to the room's rear window and looked down at my rented car, parked at the end of the driveway. Then I moved to the side window, the one that overlooked the neighboring property. Miss Blaisdell was down there in her backyard vegetable garden, tying up what looked like tomato plants. Hoping to catch her before she went back into her house, I brushed my teeth in the bathroom at the old washbasin, with its network of fine cracks, and hastily dressed. She was still in her garden when I went out the back door into my own yard. I greeted her over the hedge. "Lovely morning, isn't it?"

"Except for the cutworms. They got two of my plants last night. Still, I've got plenty yet. You like vine-ripened tomatoes?"

"Who doesn't?"

"I should have some for you pretty soon."

She talked on for a few minutes about the joys and sorrows of gardening. When she paused for breath I managed to say, "Miss Blaisdell, I've been wondering about something. It's this house. Has it always been here?"

Her expression said she had begun to wonder if I were a bit cracked. "The one you rented? Of course not. Must have been bare land there before somebody built on it, oh, say a hundred and sixty, seventy years ago."

"That's not what I meant. Could the house have been moved here from somewhere else? I saw an old photograph in the *Messenger* window of a house being moved."

"It looked like the one you are in now?"

"No, not at all. But I got to thinking. This house is—different from the others along here. Set farther back from the street, for one thing."

It was a weak reason for thinking that the house might have been moved here from someplace else, but she seemed to accept it. "Well, all I know is it's been right there as long as I can remember, and I'm eighty-two."

I hadn't realized she was that old.

"But wait a minute. Now that I think of it, my mother told me something about the house next door being moved from somewhere else. Seems to me she said it happened before any of my older brothers and sisters were born. That would put it back to around eighteen-ninety, say.

"She kept a scrapbook," Miss Blaisdell went on, "the way a lot of people did before there was entertainment like TV or radio or even movies. If it was in the paper, she might have clipped it out. Anyway, I'll get her scrapbook down from the attic and look through it."

"I don't like to put you to any trouble. After all, it's just my idle curiosity."

She put her head to one side, like an inquisitive bird. "Be funny, though, if your hunch about that house is right. Mighty funny, you being new here, I mean."

"Yes." Then, not wanting to pursue the topic: "Well, I haven't had breakfast. See you later, Miss Blaisdell."

I saw Martin twice more during the next few days. He took me out for another excellent dinner, this time at a noisy, crowded Amagansett restaurant aptly called The Boiler Room.

The next afternoon he took me along with him when he showed several of those staggeringly expensive houses behind the Bridgehampton dunes to a famous Hollywood star and his girlfriend. What he wanted, the actor said, was a place where he could spend a day or two now and then whenever he made a picture on the East Coast. He was short, perhaps five-feet-seven, in what may have been elevator shoes. But he didn't seem short, because every one of those inches carried the authority of a man whose price was ten million a picture, up front.

None of the first three houses was to his liking. At the first house he stood in the center of the vast, cathedral-ceilinged living room, his expression indicating that he alone of the four of us detected something unpleasant in the air, perhaps the odor of a dead raccoon under the house. Finally he said a single word, "No," and strode toward the door.

At the next two houses his objections were fairly detailed. Only one Jacuzzi for a house this size? Surely the guest rooms as well as the master bedroom should have breakfast terraces. And that swimming pool! He hadn't known that they still made rectangular pools for private residences. Owl-eyed behind his glasses, often leaning against a wall or mantelpiece, Martin offered agreement to many of the star's criticisms, and only mild rebuttal to others.

As for the actor's girlfriend, she was a small brunette, cute rather than beautiful, with sloe eyes, a straight little nose, and an appealing hint of overbite. She had said, "How do you do?" during the introductions in Martin's office, and not a word since. But several times I saw her throw an interested side glance, not at her own multi-millionaire boyfriend, but at my own lanky and laconic companion. To my dismay, I felt not detached amusement but something uncomfortably akin to jealousy.

As we entered the fourth house, a vaguely Moorish structure of white stucco, Martin said, "I'm sure you won't like this one. But since you can spare a few more minutes, maybe you'd want to give it a glance."

55

The actor gave it more than that. Not waiting for Martin to show the way, he strolled like a pocket-sized John Wayne from room to room, with the rest of us trailing him. Maybe he really did take a fancy to the house. Or maybe Martin's unorthodox salesmanship had worked. Or maybe he too had observed those interested looks his girl had been giving Martin. Whatever the reason, he finally said, "You're dead wrong. I like this house. Too bad you wasted time taking me to those other places. My business manager will be in touch."

Outside, the actor and his girlfriend drove off in a black Porsche toward East Hampton. Martin and I took a road that led through a potato field, its white blossoms dyed faint pink by near-sunset light, and then turned north toward Hampton Harbor and the house on Converse Street. Suddenly, I felt almost overwhelmed by a need to tell him what had happened to me, or had seemed to happen, in that house. But no. I could not bear the thought of the shock, or pity, or downright repugnance I might see in his face.

I spent the next few days alone, swimming at Long Beach, looking through shops in Hampton Harbor, and, with drawing pad and charcoal pencil, visiting ocean beaches, where I tried—and failed—to catch in my drawings the way light ran like quicksilver along the bending blades of the dune grass. Although Martin's prospective buyers were keeping him busy not only in the daytime but in the evenings, he telephoned me almost every day.

On an evening about two weeks after I had come to Hampton Harbor, I was later getting back to the house than I had planned. I had lingered too long in an Amagansett art gallery, and thus found myself part of the end-of-the-weekend traffic inching its way, a car length at a time, toward the expressway to New York. It was near sunset when I finally turned right onto a road that led to Hampton Harbor.

Leaving the car in the drive when I arrived, I unlocked the front door and went into the house. Because the little hall had already filled with shadows, I switched on the amber wall lights. I would set a place at the dining room table and then go into the kitchen to concoct a tuna salad with the vegetables I had bought at a farm stand. I placed my straw shoulder bag beside the phone on the hall table and then opened the dining room door.

Samuel sat at one end of the rectangular, white-clothed table, his massive head silhouetted against the reddish sunset light coming through the window behind him. The glow of the branched silver candelabra standing at the table's center glistened on his black-bearded face. As I often did, I wondered why hair grew so luxuriantly on his face and so sparsely on his head. Only a few strands, carefully combed from ear to ear, lay as if plastered onto his skull.

He placed his spoon beside his soup bowl. "Madam, at what hour do we have supper at this time of the year?"

"At half after six, Samuel." Quickly I slipped into my chair and took my napkin from its pewter ring.

"When you hung up your cloak and bonnet in the hall, did you happen to look at the clock?"

"Yes. I saw it was a quarter of seven."

"Well?"

"I have been visiting Nora Bradfield. I could not get away."

The door to the kitchen opened and Callie, Sara's somewhat younger sister, came in with my bowl of soup. She was shorter and slighter than her sister, and yet they looked so much alike that sometimes in a dim light I mistook one for the other. Samuel had bought them both at an auction down in Baltimore years ago, soon after he married his first wife.

Callie placed my soup bowl before me. Neither of us spoke, but I could tell by the covert sympathy in her wrinkled face that she knew Samuel was displeased with me.

When she had left the room he said, "Why is it that you could not get away from the Bradfields? Did they lock you in? Command their hounds to fall upon you if you tried to walk to your carriage?"

"No." But Nora had clung to my hand with her fevered one,

57

her white face mutely pleading with me not to leave. "It is just," I said, "that Nora has fallen very ill since the stillbirth of her last child."

"In what respect is she ill?"

"She has milkleg."

"A not uncommon female complaint after childbirth, I have heard."

"Samuel, Nora is going to die!"

I had spoken more sharply than I had intended. He regarded me silently for a moment. Often I had reflected that one would have expected a man of his temperament to have small, hooded eyes. Instead they were large and dark brown and coldly lustrous.

"At least she can die knowing that she has done her duty to her husband." Realizing what was to come, I nervously spooned my soup. "To how many children has she given birth?"

"Thirteen." The last two had been stillborn. Five others had not lived beyond their second year.

"Thirteen! Thomas Bradfield has been indeed a fortunate man. Whereas I," he said, with cold fury mounting in his voice, "had no children at all from my first wife. Until the day of her death, all I got from her were complaints and sniveling.

"As for you, madam,"—I could tell by the way he spaced his words that he had become very angry indeed—"what have I gotten from you? In seven years of marriage, one puny daughter."

My own anger was rising now, an anger I dared not express. I thought of Charity upstairs in her little bed, with her nurse Flora McClintock sitting beside her. I had wanted to kiss my daughter good night, but aware that I was late for supper I had felt it wiser not to take the time.

I said, in as mild a tone as I could muster, "Our daughter is not a puny child. She is quite healthy." I pictured her bright face in its halo of dark curls, her brown eyes brimming with glee. Somehow, I felt, she had been born with the gift of happiness.

How I prayed that, when she was a little older, that gift would not be dashed from her hands.

Callie came in just then and removed Samuel's empty soup bowl and my almost untouched one. She returned within seconds and set down before Samuel the mutton joint and its surrounding roast potatoes and carrots. He waited until we were alone. Then he picked up the bone-handled carving knife in one hand and its matching fork in the other, and looked at me with cold intensity.

"Whether puny or not, she is still a female. A man wants sons, Martha! Why else do you think I have acquired these whaleships? Why else am I building a new house down on Main Street?"

For your own satisfaction, I wanted to say, but of course did not. Instead I stole a look at my reflection in the mirror above the mahogany sideboard. I looked pale. In my haste to remove my bonnet and get to the dinner table, I had disarranged a lock of the blonde hair I wore drawn back into a knot at the nape of my neck.

"A man wants sons to take his place some day." Vigorously he sawed at the joint, then laid a mutton slice on the topmost of the two plates in front of him. "May I remind you, my dear Martha, that soon you will be twenty-five? Twenty-five! Not many wives of that age in this village have failed to produce a son."

I thought, just what do you expect me to do about it? Perhaps the question somehow communicated itself to him, because he said, "It might be better if you guarded your health more carefully. All this traipsing about!"

I did not point out that, except for visiting Nora Bradfield today and going to church last Sunday, I had not been away from the house for at least ten days. He already knew that.

Stretching his long arm, he handed me my plate of mutton and vegetables. I could tell that some of his wrath had been discharged. As he cut his own slice from the joint his movements were less agitated. For a few minutes we ate in silence.

59

Then he said, "John Eldritch brought me his bill today." Eldritch was the carpenter Samuel had hired to put new roofs on the slave cabins behind the house. "He wanted to charge me seven dollars. Seven!"

There were only two cabins. One was occupied by Sara and Callie, and the other by Hannibal, who had served as a harpooner aboard one of Samuel's whaleships until he had grown too old for the work. Now in his seventies, he served as a handyman around the house and yard.

The other two domestics were Fergus and Flora McClintock. In return for my husband's payment of their passage from Scotland, they had contracted to work seven years for him. They still had four years' service to fulfill. They were both red-haired and blue-eyed, and looked so much alike that one might have thought them brother and sister.

They lived in one big room above the carriage house. For a while their little boy, now almost five, had lived with them. But when Samuel informed her that she was to be nursemaid to Charity, Flora had arranged for their son James to live with distant relatives in Flanders, a village about fifteen miles away. It would be hard for her to perform her duties and take care of her son too, she had said. I knew that was only part of the reason. She must have noticed how my husband's eyes, with bitter resentment as well as envy in their depths, had followed the red-haired little boy as he played in front of the carriage house.

Probably, too, the McClintocks had not liked the idea of their son growing older in a household where the other servants were outright slaves, not bond servants. In Hampton Harbor the attitude toward slavery was ambiguous. Putting a slave to work aboard a whaler, with his owner pocketing his earnings, was considered permissible. But the townspeople looked askance at those few families whose households were staffed by slaves.

"Seven dollars!" Samuel repeated. "And it took him only a week to do the job."

60

I thought, but Eldritch had to supply the shingles.

"I told him I'd pay him four dollars, take it or leave it, and if he went on complaining he'd never get another day's work from me. He took the four dollars."

Samuel's ill temper seemed to have worked itself out entirely. When Callie had taken our dinner plates away and brought us suet pudding, he said, "Did you see the flag on the mill this afternoon?" When a flag flew from a grist mill on high ground above the town it meant a ship was entering the harbor.

"No." I had been too distressed over my friend Nora to notice much else. "What ship is it?"

"The *Elmer Kernshaw.*" Not one of Samuel's ships then. "The captain says that when he put into Rio de Janeiro he found the *Unicorn* there, waiting for a new mizzen mast. The old one was almost carried away while they were rounding the Horn."

I kept my head down, hoping that he would not see the flush I felt burning my cheeks. Oh, thank God! The *Unicorn* once more had survived despite the typhoons and hidden reefs of the South Pacific whaling grounds, despite the perennial gales howling through the Straits of Magellan. Jared was back on the Atlantic Coast again, heading for home port.

"One of the wisest things I ever did," my husband said, "was to hire that Jared Cantrell. He's the best young captain sailing out of the Harbor, or out of New Bedford or Nantucket, for that matter.

"The *Kernshaw's* captain said that *Unicorn* had filled its holds with whale oil before it even left the South Pacific. No need to fish on this coast, which means it could be here in ten days, or thereabouts."

So soon, so soon. I sat there, half faint with desire. I could almost feel Jared's arms around me and his warm mouth pressing down on mine.

Jared was so—alive! I thought of how it had felt to tangle my fingers in his curling dark brown hair. My hands had experienced an actual tingling sensation.

I became aware of silence settling down in the room, now

illuminated only by candlelight. Apprehensively I looked at my husband, but his gaze was neither suspicious nor resentful. I almost wished it had been.

Perhaps without him realizing it he had sensed the desire pulsing through my body and had been stirred by it.

"My dear, you look somewhat tired." His voice held a familiar slight thickening. "You had best retire early. I should too. I will tell Callie to summon the others immediately to evening prayers in the parlor. Then you and I will go up to bed."

For one dangerous moment hot rebellion filled me. I wanted to shout, "No!" Instead I stood up and said, "No need for Callie to tell Flora. I'll tell her. I'll kiss Charity good night and then come down to the parlor."

He said, with an amiability that was as familiar to me as the slight thickening of his voice and the added luster in his eyes, "Very well, my dear."

I went out into the hall, started toward the foot of the stairs. Then I stopped short. I felt a surge of my heartbeats, heard a roaring in my ears.

This dim amber glow filling the hallway. It came from the electric lights in their brackets. Through that glow I stared at my shoulder bag, sitting beside the telephone.

I knew that if I turned back into the dining room now I would see no branched candelabra, no Samuel Fitzwilliam seated at the far end of the rectangular table, spooning the last of his dessert into his mouth. Instead, once I touched the wall switch, I would see an unoccupied room, furnished with a round golden oak table under a circa 1930 glass shaded hanging light.

And yet it still seemed to me, at least for that moment, that the room with the rectangular mahogany table was just as real as the one with the round oak one, and that the young woman I had been a moment ago—Martha Fitzwilliam, with her gross husband, her child, and her aching need for her absent lover—was just as real as the self who had grown up in an old Manhattan apartment and a cottage on the Jersey shore.

And, I thought bleakly, that probably meant that I was quite, quite mad.

I would not think about it now. For one thing, I felt too exhausted to think. Whatever Martha was—a young woman who had once lived, or just a creature of my disordered imagination—those repressed emotions of hers seemed to have taken a toll from my body.

I picked up my shoulder bag and climbed the stairs, somehow sure that the wallpaper in my room would be silvery gray with blue flowers, not dark brown with pink cabbage roses.

Nine

✤

Sunlight warm against my eyelids woke me. Barefoot, I walked to the window and looked down at Miss Blaisdell's cottage. It was not until then that I realized that the window of the dining room on the floor below me faced south, just as this window did. Yet in that eerie interlude last night, Samuel's massive head had been silhouetted against the reddish sunset glow in the western sky. If those moments had had any reality outside of my own mind, then it must be that this house *had* been picked up at some time in the past, moved to its present site, and set down so that its front door faced south, toward the street. And that meant, of course, that its former site had been on a street that ran at a right angle to this one.

Monroe Street ran at a right angle to Converse Street.

Miss Blaisdell had come around the corner of her house, face shadowed by a floppy straw hat. Pulse rapid, I put on shorts, pulled a sleeveless blouse over my head. I needed to get down into my own yard right away. If she went into her house too soon, I would have to knock on her door to get the information I needed. And I didn't want her to know that the answer to my question was that important to me.

I need not have pondered how to ask the question casually. I did not have to ask it at all. At the sight of me Miss Blaisdell said, "There you are! I found it."

"Found it?"

"My mother's scrapbook. Now wait right here."

She laid down her clippers and moved briskly to the front door. I waited, looking at, but not really seeing, a robin who hopped over Miss Blaisdell's lawn, trailed by two oversized offspring demanding to be fed.

My neighbor hurried toward me, clutching a large leather-bound scrapbook, with her bent finger marking the place. She opened the book, handed it to me.

The left-hand page held a photograph, faded to brown, of three pompadoured young women in long skirts and high-necked shirtwaists, arms draped around each other in one of the classical poses popular in the late nineteenth century. Written below it in white ink were the words, "Clarabelle, Rosemary, and Edith. The three Graces. April 2, 1892."

The photograph on the right-hand page showed a two-story house I instantly recognized perched on a platform which rested on two huge rollers. Evidently the mules or horses which had drawn the house to its new site had been unhitched, but their probable driver, a tall thin man with a luxuriant mustache and a self-important expression, leaned against the platform, arms crossed.

Below it someone, presumably Miss Blaisdell's mother, had written in the same hand as on the opposite page, "Now we have new neighbors! April 30, 1892."

I said, trying to sound casual, "So this house *was* moved here." I handed the scrapbook back to her. "I suppose you still have no idea where its former location was."

"No. Could of been almost anyplace. People were always shifting houses around in those days. But isn't it funny how you, a total stranger to the village, got the notion the house might have been moved here from someplace else?"

"Yes, it does seem odd."

"Couldn't be you're one of those psychics, could it?" She laughed to show she was joking.

I too laughed. "Not that I know of."

"That sort of thing is pretty popular these days, I hear, just as it was in my mother's time. She used to reminisce about it. Mediums and all that. These days they call them channelers. There's even a store here in the Harbor that sells incense and charms and books on astrology and whatnot. They call it Psychedelia, or something like that."

Martin had mentioned such a shop. I said, "Thanks for showing me the scrapbook, Miss Blaisdell. Well, I came down here to see if I left my jacket in my car. I'd better do that, and then get breakfast and go to the supermarket."

Aware of her scrutiny, I walked to my car, opened its front door, and then closed it. I waved to her and walked into the house. In the kitchen I drank a cup of instant coffee—all I had appetite for—and then decided I might as well really go to the market. I would soon need groceries. Besides, I might be able to think more clearly away from this house.

I was wheeling my sparsely filled cart down the aisle between pet foods and household aids when I almost literally ran into Martin. He carried one of the store's red shopping baskets. As nearly as I could tell, it held nothing but yogurt containers and bottled tonic water.

He said, stopping short, "Hello, there." Then he frowned. "Good Lord! What's the matter?"

I stiffened. "What do you mean?"

"You look like hell, that's what I mean."

"Sorry."

"Don't get sore. You look beautiful. It's just—are you feeling sick or something?"

"No. The trouble is I don't sleep well in hot weather." Too late, I realized that the weather had not been at all hot. In fact, for early July it had been quite cool.

If he noticed the illogic of my reply, he gave no sign of it. He said, "I've got a slew of appointments today. But tomorrow is

Tuesday. Tuesdays are always slow, because by then even the New Yorkers who've given themselves a long weekend have gone back to the city. Maureen can take care of the office tomorrow." Maureen, I gathered, was the middle-aged brunette I had seen in his office that first afternoon. "What I mean is, would you like to go clamming tomorrow?"

"Clamming?"

"You know. Digging clams. You cook them, or eat them raw. Either way, they're good for you. Better than some of that stuff you have in your basket. What's that in the white paper? Stuff from the deli department?"

"Cold cuts."

"I thought so."

"I don't like——" I almost had said I did not like cooking in hot weather. Instead I said, "I don't feel like cooking tonight."

"Do you think you'll feel like clamming tomorrow?"

I knew I should make some excuse. In my present confused and anxious state, I might tell him everything. Not just what had happened—or seemed to me to have happened—in that rented house. I might find myself talking of the clinic, and of Victor, and of my mother and Aunt Louise and the alcoholic haze in which they had passed days and weeks and years in that high-ceilinged old apartment.

I might even talk of Samuel Fitzwilliam.

And I did not want to. If I did tell him all that, surely he would regret having had anything to do with me. And even if I never saw him again after this moment when we stood here, between the cans of Alpo and the plastic bottles of Clorox, I wanted him to retain a good opinion of me.

He said, "I'll pick you up at two tomorrow? Okay?"

I heard myself saying, "Okay."

"Great. Well, I'd better pick up some breakfast food. See you tomorrow." He headed toward the cereals, and I toward the check-out counter.

A few minutes later I placed two tall bags of groceries in the trunk of my car and then stood motionless. There it was, directly opposite: the office of the *Messenger*. I closed the trunk and then crossed the street.

Inside, a half dozen or so men and women sat at desks lining the walls. A red-haired young woman got up from the first desk on the right and walked toward me, smiling. "May I help you?"

"I hope so. Do you have back copies of the *Messenger?*"

"We certainly do. Our files go clear back to the first edition in 1857. And it's all on microfilm." The pride in her voice made me think that the microfilming had been done recently. "What period are you interested in?"

"April, 1892."

"Well, I'm afraid I can't let you use the machine. Somebody came in off the street a few weeks ago and managed to get the projector jammed, so now the publisher has said nobody but staff members can use it. But if you'll tell me what you want to look up—"

"A—a house that was moved to a location on Converse Street. I want to know what its previous location was."

From her expression I gathered that house moving was about the last thing she had thought I might be researching. "I'll see what I can find. Why don't you wait at my desk?" She walked toward a door at the far end of the room.

A copy of Fodor's *Guide to New York State* lay on her desk. As I leafed through the Long Island section of the book, I thought of how both Martin and Miss Blaisdell had said that there was much interest in psychic phenomena here in the Hamptons. There was even a shop in this village which specialized in books on the supernatural, as well as such paraphernalia as crystals.

The red-haired girl had returned. "I looked through all four weekly issues for April, 1892, and through the last two issues for March and the first two for May, and there wasn't a single item about a house moving." She paused. "That doesn't mean there weren't any. I've heard that back then people used to move houses at the drop of a hat. Maybe house moving just stopped being news."

"Maybe." But I had thought that anything concerning that particular house might be considered news, even decades after its first notoriety. I said, "I guess you don't have any records going back beyond 1857."

"That's right. Did something happen back then, something you're interested in, I mean?"

I couldn't discuss with a stranger what might have occurred in that house in 1840, particularly a stranger whose eyes held such avid curiosity.

"No, not anything in particular." I had intended to ask her the location of that shop both Martin and Miss Blaisdell had mentioned, but now I thought better of it. In a town this small, I should have little difficulty finding any shop. I added, "Thank you for your time and trouble."

I left the building, turned to my right. I passed an antique shop, a deli, another antique shop. There it was above a narrow doorway, a sign in Gothic script that said "Psychedelia."

I left the sidewalk and climbed steep old stairs. No wonder, I thought, that people of past centuries had tended to die young. They must have worn themselves out climbing stairs with foot-high risers. At the top of the stairs a door stood open.

Inside the shop a young man arranging crystal pendants on a table straightened up and smiled at me. He wore faded jeans and a yellow turtleneck, and he was so good-looking—with his curly blond hair and tanned, chiseled features—that I was sure he was an aspiring actor. "Greetings," he said. "What can I do for you?"

Feeling oddly embarrassed, I asked, "Do you have books on reincarnation?"

He looked at the book shelves that ran from the floor almost to the ceiling along one wall. "Reincarnation, reincarnation. Well, I know we're out of Shirley MacLaine's latest. We can't keep her in stock. But we do have books on Hinduism. Reincarnation is part of their religion, of course. Why don't you just browse?"

He turned around to transfer one of the crystal pendants to

a table holding incense burners in the shape of pagodas. I saw that those artfully faded jeans had been designed by Calvin Klein. He said, turning back, "We have books on astrology, witchcraft, palmistry, Tarot cards, the whole field of psychic phenomena. I'm sure you'll find something to interest you."

"All right." I walked over to the bookshelves. After a while I took down a book entitled *You and Your Past Lives.* It began, "Remember when you were very young, and first read stories about King Arthur and Queen Guinevere and the Knights of the Round Table? You thought of how wonderful it would have been to live in their time. Well, dear reader, perhaps you did." I thrust the book back into place and took down one entitled, *Key to Hinduism.* If the first book had been too childish, this one—evidently a translation from the original Hindustani— was too abstruse, made up of non-stop sentences and unfamiliar proper names that usually started with a "K" and sometimes stretched halfway across a page.

I replaced that book too and turned around. "Thank you, but I'm afraid—"

"Dear, I just thought of something. I think that Paul—he owns this shop—has an old copy of *The Search for Bridey Murphy* in the back room. Shall I go and look? Oh, that must have been well before your time. Before mine too, really, but maybe you've heard of it."

"Yes. I also heard it was proved to be a hoax."

"Then you don't want me to look for it?"

"No, thank you."

He hesitated. "Would you mind telling me why you asked for a book on reincarnation?"

I said, feeling suddenly depressed, "I'm just—curious."

"But you don't believe in it, do you? As soon as you walked in I thought, 'She doesn't look the type.' Well, I don't believe in it either. I think it's all crap."

"What is?"

He waved a long-fingered hand to indicate the whole shop.

70

"Astrology, reincarnation, all of it. And I'll bet you agree, don't you?"

I gave a forced, noncommittal smile.

Once, I would have agreed with him. I wished that I could agree now. But if I could—if what I had experienced in that house hadn't really happened—then where did that leave me? It left me, obviously, as someone who should still be a patient at the Morse-Whitlow Clinic.

In my depressed state I needed to lash out at someone, and so I said, "If you feel that way, why do you work here?"

"To support myself, of course, while I do my real work. I act. I played the newsboy in *Streetcar* at Guild Hall last month. I know, I'm a bit old for the part, but I think I got away with it. And soon I'll play the Englishman in 'California Suite.' A group in Westhampton is presenting it."

"But don't you feel uncomfortable about working here?"

"Oh, my conscience is clear. I've memorized all the patter about sun signs and out-of-body experiences and all the rest of it. I give good value, just as I did last year in a golf club pro shop, where I talked about grips and follow-throughs with all these Rotary Club types."

"Well, goodbye. And thank you."

"Not at all, dear. Come back soon. We get in new books all the time."

A few minutes later I stopped in the driveway of my rented house and carried my groceries in through the back door. I began to put them away in the cupboard and refrigerator. Again I was struck with how ordinary-looking this house was, with its worn appliances, its linoleum of the same pattern of colored dots—confetti pattern, my mother had called it—which had been in that summer cottage on the Jersey shore. But the house no longer seemed to me in the least ordinary. I had a sense of lives other than my own solitary one moving just below the surface like an underground stream, lives that presumably had ended many decades ago.

I thought of Samuel's massive head silhouetted against the

sunset glow beyond that dining room window. I thought of Martha's face reflected in the sideboard mirror. Hers was a face trained not to show emotion. But I had firsthand knowledge of her emotions, the fear and loathing her husband aroused in her, and her aching need to be in her lover's arms.

Strange. During those intervals when I seemed to move about this house as Martha Fitzwilliam, I had had no sense even of the existence of Gail Loring, a young woman who, in the closing years of the twentieth century, would rent this house for the summer. By contrast, I could remember every detail of my moments as Martha. The reason wasn't hard to see. She could have no consciousness of me, any more than of computers or rock music or feminism, because she had died many decades before I was born.

Unless—and here it was again, that chilling unless—unless it was only in my sick fancy that I had moved about this house with blonde hair drawn back into a knot and muslin skirts sweeping the floor.

I stared dully at the canned goods I had placed on a cupboard shelf. I did not feel hungry. But having skipped breakfast, I could not skip lunch too. I took down a can of chicken soup and reached into a drawer for the can opener.

*T*en

The stretch of Noyac Bay shoreline where Martin and I went clamming the next day wasn't good for much else. Except for a narrow strip of sand close inshore, the beach was covered with large pebbles and broken clam and mussel shells. To find water deep enough for swimming one would have to wade out about a hundred yards over rock-and-shell-strewn tidal flats. Consequently, the only people in sight when we drove up to the parking area above the beach were two clammers—probably professionals, Martin said—who plied their clam rakes in chest-deep water. At that distance their figures looked black against the dazzling blue bay.

We got out of Martin's car, he in yellow surfer's shorts, I in a dark blue cotton bikini. So that I would not cut my feet on the rocks and broken shells, Martin had brought along well worn sneakers for me. I found them a fairly good fit. Probably I was far from the first date he had taken clamming. Again, as when I caught that actor's girlfriend giving Martin interested looks, I felt a distinct twinge of jealousy.

He had also brought two clamming baskets, ordinary bushel

baskets set inside inflated inner tubes. "So the baskets will float," he explained. He brought only one clam rake, an iron tool with curved steel claws and a five-foot-long wooden handle. "I didn't bring one for you. You'd never be able to lift it up through several feet of water, especially since it would be holding sand and rocks and maybe clams. You'd better clam with your feet."

"My feet?"

"When you get out to where the bottom is sandy, take off your sneakers and tie them around your neck. Then dig your toes into the sand. When you feel something hard, crouch down and dig it out with your fingers. Most of the time it'll be a rock, but now and then it should be a clam."

There were cords attached to the basket handles. We knotted the other ends around our waists. Then, with the baskets trailing behind us, we waded through sun-warmed water. At last Martin said, "This ought to be about right for you." The rocks and broken shells underfoot had given way to soft sand.

While his hand under my elbow supported me, I took off the sneakers. I knotted their laces around my neck and then felt around in the sand with my toes.

"I've got one!"

I crouched chin-deep in water, grasped a hard object, brought it to the surface. It was a pink, brown-speckled rock about the size and shape of a duck's egg.

"Keep trying," he said. "You'll have better luck. I'm going out to where it's deeper."

My luck did change. The very next try I came up with a clam that turned out to be the biggest either of us caught. Soon my toes and fingers could tell the difference between a rock and the ridged surface of a clam's shell. I collected a dozen, and then decided to call it a day.

Eyes closed, I floated on my back, aware of the tug of the cord tied around my waist. After a while, gently rocked by the bay's currents, warmed by the sun, I began to feel a sense of timelessness. For a blessed interval all that troubled me seemed to vanish. No, not vanish. My memories of that New Jersey afternoon, my bewilderment over what had happened to me, or seemed to have happened, in the house I now occupied— all that was still there beneath the level of my consciousness. But on the surface I was aware only of the water's gentle rocking, and the sun's heat, and the mewling of some seabird.

"Did pretty well, didn't you? You must have caught about a dozen."

I opened my eyes, smiled up at Martin. "An even dozen," I said, and stood up.

"Good. I got about twice that. We'll have plenty for chowder."

We put the two baskets in the car trunk. Then, on the narrow stretch of sand above the rocky tidal flats, we lay down to dry ourselves in the sun. For a while there was silence. Then Martin turned over. Leaning on his elbows, he looked down at me.

"All right. Tell me about it. And don't say about what. I want to know what was wrong with you in the supermarket yesterday. You seem a little better today, but not much. So what's wrong?"

When I didn't answer he went on, "You seemed pretty much okay that first day in my office. A little jumpy, maybe. You seemed pretty much okay the night we went to the Wharf Club, too. But yesterday, and today again—"

I thought, with reckless despair, Why not tell him? I had wanted to keep his respect, but what good would it do me, since there could never be anything serious between us. How could there be, with my heritage? And so why not at least give myself the relief of leveling with him?

I began to talk. I told it all in a jumble, starting with Victor, and then moving back to that afternoon with Aunt Louise on the porch of that New Jersey cottage, and then forward to my stay at the clinic, and then back to my mother's swift descent into alcoholism, and then, once more, back to what Aunt Louise had said about my Hampton Harbor ancestor.

I stopped speaking. He still looked down at me. Despite his

dark glasses, I could see that his eyes were troubled indeed. His voice, though, was terse and noncommittal. "All right. But all that was in the past. What's changed you in the last few days?"

"That—that house."

"The house you rented?" I nodded. "What about the house?"

I told him. Before I had spoken more than a few sentences he lay down on his back and put his forearm across his eyes. I knew he was listening, though, and so I plowed doggedly on.

At last he said, his arm still covering his eyes, "And how do you explain all this?"

I blurted out, "I think that when that house was built it was on Monroe Street."

"I suppose that's possible. As I told you, in the old days moving houses around was a favorite Hampton Harbor sport."

I thought of the first day I had peered through the mesh curtains into that small parlor. Certainly it was not an attractive room. And yet I had felt drawn to it, almost as if it were inviting me inside.

I spoke with a rush. "I had a sense that the house recognized me."

I hadn't known I was going to say that. And I wished that I had not. Then I told myself that it didn't matter, not after all the other things I had told him.

He sat up. "I want you to get out of that house." He looked at his watch. "Almost four-thirty. If we go there now, and you pack, and start driving to New York—"

"Why? Why do you want me out of there? Is it because you think that what happened to me was—real?"

"No!" His voice was harsh.

I said flatly, "Then you think I'm insane."

"No! I don't know what is true. I just know you should get out of that house and out of Hampton Harbor entirely. I'll see that you get a refund, although it may take a little time." Again he looked at his watch. "If you don't get away from here within an hour, you'll be driving part of the way in the dark. Maybe you'd better go to a motel tonight, and then drive to the city first thing in the morning."

My voice sounded thick. "So you're that eager to get rid of me." Well, I had realized what his reaction might be. Why hadn't I kept to my resolution not to tell him?

"It's not that! Don't you realize I'd turn this town upside down to try to find another rental for you? Or I'd be glad— more than glad!—to have you stay at my place. But what you need is counseling, the sooner the better. You need that woman doctor, the one you told me about."

"She's on Cape Cod."

"Then someone else on the clinic staff. They can't all be on Cape Cod. Gail, listen to me. I'm worried about you. And the worst of it is that I won't be here for the next ten days. I've got to go to Albany. The state university is holding a conference, and English department faculty members of every branch of the university are obligated to attend. It may cost me my job if I'm not there. So please, Gail—"

"Go to your conference. You have no reason in the world to stay away on my account. You know about me now. At least two generations of alcoholics behind me—"

"Maybe I don't have reason to care that much." His voice was matter-of-fact. "But I find that I do. As for alcoholism, my God, girl. Don't you realize that almost everyone, myself included, has a lush or two in his family?"

I thought, it wasn't just fear of inherited alcoholism. It was fear that I had landed in Morse-Whitlow Clinic, not just because of an unhappy love affair, but because of a mind sickness I might have inherited from a man who lived a century and a half ago, a sickness that had exploded into some terrible act of violence.

True, a century and a half was a long time. Perhaps if I had not moved into that house on Converse Street, Samuel Fitzwilliam would have remained for me a shadowy figure, an ancestor too remote for him to cause me more than an uneasy thought now and then.

But he no longer seemed remote. Samuel, with his coldly lustrous brown eyes and curly black beard, was almost as real to me as the lanky man lying propped on his elbows beside me. I had to try to learn why that was so. Was I just an incipient crazy who already had been hospitalized once? Or were these phantoms in some sense real—Samuel, and the three aged blacks, and the blonde woman through whose eyes I looked at a world of giant clothes presses and kitchen fireplaces and wooden-handled sink pumps?

Maybe I would never learn the truth. But I had to try. I felt that otherwise I simply could not get on with my life.

"You can't order me out of that house," I said with dull stubbornness. "I gave you my check."

He looked down at me for a long moment. I saw at least momentary defeat in his eyes before he put it into words. "All right. Then stay in the house." He got to his feet. "We'd better go now. It takes time to cook clam chowder."

"Chowder?"

"Don't you remember? I said I'd cook chowder for us. I've got a clam knife and chopping bowl in the car trunk, along with onions and potatoes.

"Besides," he added grimly. "I want to spend a little time in that house. I've never been in it for more than a few minutes at a stretch."

Two and a half hours later we sat at the round oak dining room table with its faux Tiffany glass shade. Martin now wore jeans and a blue tee shirt. While I waited in the car, he had gone to his apartment above the real estate office to change. As for me, I had gone upstairs as soon as we reached the house, leaving him to start cooking while I showered and changed into my yellow cotton dress.

As I took my first sip of the steaming chowder Martin had set before me, I thought of how the room had looked when the table was a mahogany rectangle with Samuel seated at one end of it, bearded face and almost bald head massive against the red sunset light.

Even before he spoke, I knew that Martin, too, was remembering my description of that scene. He said, "Do you feel it now—right now—that sense of something strange about this house?"

I shook my head. From the moment we had come through the back door, he carrying the basket of clams and I the other ingredients, I had felt the difference in the atmosphere. I no longer had a sense of past time moving beneath the present, like an underground stream. It was Martin's presence, I felt, that made that difference.

He went on, "No westward-facing window in this room? No black slaves in the kitchen?" He tried to speak lightly, but I could tell he was still both concerned and angry.

"No."

After a moment he went on, "It's unlikely that there were ever slaves in this house. Some men bought slaves to send on whaling voyages, but there were very few house slaves."

"Yes," I said vaguely. Then, to change the subject: "The chowder is a great success."

"Thank you. They say the Indians taught the Pilgrims to make chowder, but it couldn't have been this kind. There were no potatoes growing in New England until someone brought some plants from Ireland in the early eighteenth century."

Throughout the rest of the meal, which included crusty bread, a lettuce salad, and fresh blueberries, Martin talked about early Long Islanders' relations—sometimes friendly, sometimes hostile—with various Indian tribes.

When the meal was over we did the dishes together. The house still seemed to hold the impersonal atmosphere of a rather shabby rental property occupied over the decades by scores of people.

Martin hung the cups he had just dried from their cupboard hooks. He looked at his watch. "I'll have to leave soon. I've arranged to pick up another teacher in Stony Brook at six tomorrow morning. But before I leave, I want to see the room with the wallpaper that changes."

His gaze was challenging. I said, "All right."

We went up the stairs. In the room I had chosen for my bedroom, I touched the wall switch. Light shone on the silver-gray paper strewn with blue flowers, on the double bed, with its inexpensive maple headboard, and the blue-skirted dressing table.

"At one time there was a fireplace right there." I pointed across the room. "You can see the outline of a chimney on the shingles outside. And when you thump the wall in here at that spot it sounds hollow."

"I'm sure it does. Gail, don't you realize that almost any house of this age once had a number of fireplaces? They were the only source of heat. When people began installing oil or coal furnaces, they blocked off most of the fireplaces so as not to lose heat up the chimneys." He gave me a baffled look. "Oh, Gail! Won't you do as I say? Go back to the city. I'll call you there. We'll—"

I shook my head.

"Damn it all!" He seized my shoulders. "Why won't you listen?"

He kissed me, not a gentle kiss this time, but prolonged, and filled with anger as well as desire. I felt a surging response. But it would be no good like this, with him angry and me confused and frightened. Oh, I knew the anger was not on his own behalf, but on mine. He was furious because I would not do what he felt was best for me. But it was anger, all the same.

I wrenched my lips free. "No, Martin."

"Then at least come back to my place for the night. Please! It's not good for you to be here."

I shook my head.

With thumb and forefinger he turned my face back toward his and again brought his mouth down on mine. I felt his other hand tug at the zipper at the back of my dress.

"No!" I got my hands up, pushed both palms against his shoulders, and broke free. He looked down at me, face flushed.

Then he made a short sound that was not quite a laugh.

"Sorry. I'm not usually like that. But when you find your way blocked by people who lived way back in the last century, if they lived at all—"

He broke off, and then added, "Good night, Gail. I'll see you when I get back."

I stood there, listening to the sound of his feet on the stairs. After an interval, I heard his car back out of the drive and turn onto the street. The sound of its engine dwindled away.

The electric wall lights still glowed. The gray and blue wallpaper remained the same. And yet I could sense the change. Beneath the present, that underground stream was again flowing.

*E*leven

🙣

The next day, after a lunch that consisted solely of clam chowder left over from the night before, I visited Hampton Harbor's two cemeteries. It was strange, I reflected, that it had not occurred to me earlier to look for my ancestor's grave.

The first cemetery I visited adjoined a white frame church. The guidebook I had bought the day after my arrival in the village said that it was popularly known as the Old Graveyard and had been opened in 1690, long before the church beside it had been built. Some of the headstones had been worn so smooth that they bore no lettering at all. Those graves, I was sure, must date from the village's earliest days. Finally I did find a section of the cemetery where all the headstones bore mid-nineteenth century dates. But I did not find Samuel Fitzwilliam's name.

A side door of the church opened and a gray-haired woman, chic in a pink linen dress and pink cardigan, approached along the graveled path. "May I help you? I'm Mrs. Maxwell, the pastor's wife."

"Gail Loring," I said, and took the hand she extended.

"In the two years my husband and I have been in this village, I've practically memorized every headstone in this cemetery. So if you are looking for some particular grave—"

I said, after a moment, "Samuel Fitzwilliam."

"An ancestor of yours?"

I nodded, unable to speak.

"Well, you won't find his grave here. Probably it's in the Fairlawn Cemetery on Cadoval Street. When the Old Graveyard became too full back around the turn of the century, a lot of graves were transferred to Fairlawn."

I thanked her and then drove to the much larger cemetery on Cadoval Street. Here an elderly man pushed a cart along one of the wide gravel paths, pausing now and then to remove fallen branchlets or withered flowers from the mounded graves. I asked him about Samuel Fitzwilliam.

"Fitzwilliam, Fitzwilliam. We've got a John Fitzwilliam. Young fella. He and his parents moved here from Brooklyn. Did a year in Vietnam without getting a scratch, and then got killed in a car smash his first week home."

"That's not the one. The Fitzwilliam I'm looking for must have died in the eighteen-hundreds."

"This cemetery wasn't opened until nineteen-oh-one, so if he's here he's over in that section." He pointed. "That's where they reburied the ones they brought over from the Old Graveyard about eighty years ago."

I searched the area he had indicated, but there was no stone for Samuel Fitzwilliam. Perhaps my ancestor had fled after committing his heinous crime, whatever it had been. If so, probably he had taken his young wife and child with him, because there were no stones for them either.

For the first time I wondered what I would have felt if I had found myself looking down at the grave of that rebellious and passionate young woman with the decorously smooth blonde hair, that woman whose very body I, for brief periods, had seemed to inhabit.

I walked down the broad main path, with its moving shadows of wind-stirred tree branches. Near the gate the elderly caretaker was trimming an ilex tree. He said, "Find it?"

I shook my head. My frustration must have been plain in my manner, because he asked, "Any other way I can help you?"

"I don't imagine so. It might help some if I could find out more about a house that was moved from one street to another here in Hampton Harbor back in the eighteen-nineties, but I'm sure you wouldn't know about that."

"No, but a housemover might."

I felt startled. "A housemover? You mean people still move houses?" Somehow I had assumed that it was only in times long past that houses had been trundled along the village streets.

"Now and then. Often enough that there's a fella who still makes a living out of it. He might be able to help you. He's a young fella, about forty-five, but the business has been in his family since his grandfather's time. Name's Bert Jeffers."

"He lives here in the village?"

"Between here and East Hampton. Has his business there too. Just drive out Route One-fourteen. Bert's place is just the other side of Hickford's Motel."

"Thank you."

Questions were gathering in his eyes. Before he could ask them I said goodbye and walked to my rented car.

A few minutes later, out on One-fourteen, I passed the motel. A semicircle of tree-shadowed gray frame cabins, it looked like something out of a nineteen-thirties movie. Just beyond it a wooden arch, bearing the words "Jeffers' Housemoving," spanned the entrance to a dirt drive. I turned under the arch. On either side of me forlorn-looking structures stood at varying angles on the bare earth.

I saw no building even approaching the size of my rented house. Instead there were garages, tool sheds, and one gray frame cottage roofed with tar paper. The road ended at the screen door of a small wooden structure with fairly fresh white paint. Above the doorway a sign said, "Office."

84

I mounted two wooden steps, knocked. Someone said, "Come in."

I opened the screen door. A man, overweight and bald, turned around in his chair from a littered knee-hole desk. "Are you Mr. Jeffers?"

"That's right." His smile was friendly enough. Apparently it was lethargy rather than surliness that kept him seated. "What can I do for you?"

"I'm afraid I'm not a customer. I'm just looking for information."

"Yeah?"

"I understand your grandfather started this business."

"That's right. And a real business it was in those days. Lots of people decided to have their houses moved."

"Why?"

"I don't know." From his tone I gathered he had never given the matter much thought. "Kind of a fad, maybe. Anyway, it stopped. About the biggest thing I move these days is a two-car garage. Now you said you wanted some information."

"About a house I've rented on Converse Street. I learned it had been moved there from somewhere else. I wondered if you might have a record of it."

"Record? Probably. The business he started don't amount to much now, but he sure did leave records. You know the date?"

"April, 1892."

Grunting a little, he bent over and pulled open the bottom drawer of his desk. As he began to take out ledgers, bound in gray cloth, and pile them on the desk, he said, "There were two other housemovers in the Harbor in those days, so maybe one of them handled the job. But Grandpop did more moving than the other two put together, so probably——"

He opened a ledger and ran a stubby finger down a page. From where I stood I could see that the ledger entries had been made in ink now faded to brown.

"This must be it. 'For moving two-story frame house from

Monroe Street to Converse Street, twenty dollars. Paid in full April 10, 1892.' "

Even though I'd been almost certain that my rented house had once stood on Monroe Street, his words carried a shock. I asked, "Is there a name?"

"Name?"

"Of whoever it was who owned the house."

"No, it was a cash deal. Grandpop wrote down the name only when there was money owing to him."

Even if there had been a name, I reflected, it probably would have told me nothing. By the time the house had been moved, Samuel Fitzwilliam's violent act was already a half-century in the past. In that span of time the house might have changed hands several times.

"Anything else I can do?"

Evidently his laziness was mental as well as physical, because I saw no curiosity in his round face. "I don't think so. But thanks very much for what you did tell me."

About ten minutes later I turned into the driveway of my rented house. Miss Blaisdell stood on her lawn, watering one of her petunia-filled window boxes with a hose. I waved.

She called, "We need rain. Says on TV that this has been the driest early summer on record."

"I'm not surprised." Feeling too tense for small talk, I smiled and then hurried across my own lawn. I opened the front door and went inside.

Evidently Callie, whose job it was to light a lamp in the windowless entrance hall in mid-afternoon, had fallen into ab-sentmindedness again, because the little entryway was filled with shadows. I sighed. I would have to reprimand her, and I never liked doing that. As I often did, I reflected that I was not cut out to be the wife of a man rich enough to keep three slaves and two bond servants.

As I hung my bonnet and cloak on the hall tree I became aware of Samuel's voice speaking behind the closed door of the west parlor. So we had a visitor. Probably it was Makepeace

86

Thorn, his closest associate and a fellow deacon of the Brethren United in Christ.

I looked at my dim reflection in the hall mirror. Some people said that blonde women faded young. Almost twenty-five, I kept expecting to see silver threads in my hair and lines at the corners of my eyes. So far that had not happened. I knew that even if Callie had not forgotten to light the lamp, I still would have seen a face little changed from what it had been when, at the age of seventeen, I had married Samuel Fitzwilliam. I smoothed my hair with both hands and then opened the parlor door.

Just inside the doorway I stopped short. Feeling that I might faint, I clung to the doorknob. My husband sat in his accustomed chair beside the fireplace, its empty grate now hidden by a large peacock-blue fan one of his ships had brought back from Hong Kong. On the opposite side of the fireplace, one elbow resting on the marble mantel, stood Jared Cantrell, skipper of the *Unicorn*. Evidently he had come straight from the ship to his employer's house, because he still wore the short, dark blue broadcloth jacket of a whaleship officer. Its brevity emphasized the width of his shoulders and the length of his legs in broadcloth trousers. His face had been browned more deeply than ever by the tropic sun. That brownness seemed to emphasize the warmth and brilliance of his hazel eyes. His hair, glossy and brown and curling, was somewhat shorter than it had been when I last saw him more than a year before, but it was still long enough that a lock of it fell over his forehead. My hand seemed to ache with the need to touch that alive, springy hair and smooth that lock back into place.

I was able to move now. I advanced into the room. "Why, Captain Cantrell! What a surprise." And it was a surprise. I had known—I had gone to sleep each night with the knowledge and awakened to it in the morning—that he was expected to drop anchor in the harbor soon, but I hadn't known it would be this soon.

I did not extend my hand. With Samuel watching me as that

warm, firm hand closed around mine, I might have betrayed myself.

Jared said, "You are looking well, Mrs. Fitzwilliam." His eyes were saying much more. Couldn't Samuel see that? I threw my husband a nervous glance, but his face was complacent, even unwontedly good-humored.

I said, "Will you be with us long, Captain?"

"That is for Mr. Fitzwilliam to say. I do hope to be here a week or more."

"You will my boy, you will," Samuel said jovially. "After all, you not only filled the holds but brought back a big sperm whale slung alongside. It will take us days to try out the blubber." He meant render the whale into oil.

"I realize that. But I hope that by Thursday I'll have leisure to hire a mount from the livery stable and visit some favorite spots around here."

I understood instantly. The old fort, whose crumbling walls were all that was left of a fortification the British had built during the Revolutionary War. On Thursday afternoon we would meet there.

Samuel was saying, "But you can't linger ashore too long, my boy. I have a feeling that whaling will be finished within a few years. Some whaling grounds already are about fished out. Besides, we keep hearing rumors that they may strike petroleum in Pennsylvania or some other place before long. Still, the *Unicorn* ought to have a few more good voyages before I either scrap her or convert her to the China trade."

Thinking of Thursday, I scarcely heard him. Thursday Jared and I would be together at the old fort where we had met the last time he was in the Harbor, and where, less than two years ago, he had for the first time kissed me and held me in his arms. At the memory the pulse in the hollow of my throat again began to beat so fast that I felt smothered.

I said, trying to speak in a normal voice, "I hope you will be able to spare time to dine with us before you leave, Captain Cantrell."

He inclined his head. "I shall look forward to it, ma'am."

"But it's time right now for you to partake of our hospitality," Samuel said. "Martha, why don't you pull the bell rope? We'll have Callie or someone bring up a bottle of the Madeira the captain likes. And she mustn't forget those English biscuits."

"I had best see to it myself." Perhaps if I were alone for a few moments, I could get better control of my feelings. "Callie might bring up the wrong bottle."

I left the parlor, closing the door behind me.

The phone on the hall table rang.

I stood stock still while the phone rang two more times. Then I lifted it from its cradle. "Hello."

"Is Timmy there?" The voice was very young—thirteen, perhaps—and very trusting, the voice of some girl who had asked a boy on the beach for his number, and perhaps received a phony one for her pains.

"I'm sorry, but I'm afraid you have the wrong number."

"Isn't this 233-9976?"

"Yes, but there is no Timmy here."

"You're sure?" Now she sounded twelve or less.

"I'm sure. I'm all alone here."

I hung up. All alone. If I walked back to the kitchen I would find no Callie, no Sara, just a well worn Hot Point range and a somewhat newer General Electric refrigerator. And that parlor? If I walked back into it I would find that a green painted wooden fireplace mantel had replaced that handsome marble one, and that where the graceful silk fan had been stood an electric heater. And there would be no one beside myself in the room.

My straw handbag rested beside the phone. I had no memory of placing it there. What I remembered was hanging up my brown merino cloak and my brown bonnet, with its taffeta ruche. Then I had smoothed my hair, looking into the mirror of the hall tree that had stood where the hall table was now.

I picked up my handbag and climbed the stairs.

*T*welve

As I look back at them, the next few days had a dreamlike quality. I remember venturing out of the house only twice. I went to the supermarket, and stocked up on powdered soup and yogurt and frozen vegetables and canned ham and such, even though I felt little appetite for food of any sort. Once I went to the Harbor Cinema, whose lobby poster boasted that it was the only theater in the Hamptons showing foreign films, and saw part of an Italian movie about railway workers. Near the end of the movie I felt too restless to sit still, and so drove back to the house.

Beneath its roof, past and present seemed at war, with the past winning. It was more often as Martha that I moved through the rooms, looking though curtains at carriages and wagons along Monroe Street, or visiting the carriage house and stable and two slave cabins at the rear of the property.

And as Martha, I had a bad quarrel with Samuel. It began over nothing of real importance. Samuel's breakfast tea was not to his liking, and so he made the familiar charge that I was "too lax" with the servants. I pointed out that neither Sara nor Callie was as young as she used to be. I always hated it when Samuel turned his ill temper on those two. Almost from the day I had come into this house as a seventeen-year-old bride, I had sensed their kindness, and their desire to be as protective of me as they could without bringing their master's wrath down on their own heads.

Samuel said, "You are quite right, madam." Sitting there at the mahogany table, I quailed inwardly. Whenever Samuel addressed me as "madam," I knew there was a storm ahead. He continued, "They are becoming useless, and so I think it best to take them south and sell them."

It was an empty threat, one he had been making for several years. Sara and Callie would not fetch enough to pay for the journey. But perhaps my impatient longing for Thursday, and the feeling of Jared's arms around me, had stretched my nerves too tightly. Anyway, I heard myself saying, "How can you even think of such a thing after all their years of service? How can you be so utterly—unfair?"

"Unfair? Is the world fair to me?" He began to pour out his grievances. The tenant of one of the buildings Samuel owned on Main Street, a grog shop keeper, was three months behind in his rent. A Philadelphia firm which supplied beef jerky for Samuel's ships had almost doubled its price. The *Patience Fitzwilliam*, a whaleship he had named after his first wife, was long overdue and presumably lost.

"I would not complain of all the hard work and worry if I had a son to take over after me." I pushed back my chair. "But without a son it all seems—Martha! Don't you dare walk out of this room."

I had almost reached the door when, with a catlike speed surprising in a middle-aged man of his bulk, he reached me and spun me about.

I cried, "Samuel, let me go!"

Instead he fastened one large hand around my throat.

I felt pain and what was worse than pain, a shutting off of life-giving air. I struggled, fingers clawing at that implacable hand. The blood pounded in my head, and a dark mist began closing in.

Then, abruptly, I found myself seated at the round, golden oak table. On it was my solitary breakfast, a half-finished bowl of cornflakes and milk. My throat still seemed to ache, but I knew that if I looked into a mirror I would see no fingermarks.

I began to feel afraid. It was more than the familiar fear of madness. I felt that the black-bearded man, whether a figment of my disordered imagination or in some sense real, could do me actual physical harm. But how much harm? Just what capabilities of evil did he represent? Perhaps the crews of ancient ships, sailing into uncharted waters, had felt as I felt now.

But these waters need not remain uncharted. True, neither cemetery had yielded any information about Samuel Fitzwilliam. But there might be official records in the village offices.

I went out into the hall. The lower shelf of the hall table held a phone book. My finger ran down the listings. Fire Department, Mayor's Office, Village Clerk—

That should be the one. I dialed. A woman's voice said, "Village Clerk's office."

"May I speak to the Village Clerk, please?"

"You are. How may I help you?"

"Do you have records going back to 1840, or maybe a few years earlier?"

"1840! That was a long time ago. Well, the answer to your question is yes and no. A lot of the village records have been lost to fires. In the eighteen-hundreds the Harbor was famous for its fires. One in the eighteen-seventies burned down half the business district and several ships tied up at the wharf. Now can you tell me what you're looking for?"

I said, after a moment, "Do you have anything concerning a Samuel Fitzwilliam, who lived here in the early part of the eighteen-hundreds?"

"Maybe. I won't know until I look."

I spelled out his name for her. "I should be able to call you back in a few minutes," she said, and hung up.

About a quarter of an hour passed before she called. She had looked through all the available files and found nothing. "Mind telling me what was so special about this Samuel Fitzwilliam?" Her voice had taken on the lightly teasing tone with which some people try to mask their curiosity. "I know he couldn't have been a local hero, because the Clio Club has written all of them up, from before the Revolution onward. So what did he do? Commit a murder or something?"

"He may have."

"You mean—really?" She sounded a bit disconcerted. "There haven't been many murders in the Harbor, only one in this century, I heard someone say the other day. And this in spite of people in East Hampton and Southampton saying we're sort of a tough town." Now her voice was touched with resentment. "But if there was an inquest or trial or anything like that, the place to look is the Suffolk County Records in Riverhead."

I thanked her, hung up, and reopened the phone book. After a while I dialed.

"Suffolk County Offices."

"I'm trying to find out about an inquest or trial that may have taken place—"

"I'll give you County Records."

A man answered. Before I had spoken more than a few sentences he said, "You'll have to come in, miss. We're not allowed to give out such information over the phone."

I hung up and sat there with my hand on the phone. Riverhead, the county seat, was about twenty-five miles away over roads clogged with summer traffic. And I felt so very tired. But perhaps in a day or two—

The phone rang under my hand, making me jump. I let it ring again before I lifted it.

Martin said, "How are you, Gail?"

"I'm fine."

"You don't sound it." I pictured the concerned eyes behind the hornrims. My heart yearned toward him. "What did you have for dinner last night?"

After a moment I said, "Broiled chicken and frozen peas." The truth was I couldn't remember eating dinner. I added quickly, "How's the conference?"

"It's okay. You were lying about dinner, weren't you?"

"Martin, I'm all *right*. I just feel a little tired, that's all."

He said quietly, "Please try to take care of yourself. Please. I'll see you as soon as I get back. Goodbye, Gail."

He hung up. I sat for a moment with the phone in my hand, and then put it back in its cradle.

I'm not sure what I did the rest of that day. Washed my hair, I think, and then late in the afternoon drove to that deserted beach where Martin and I had clammed. I remember wondering if people had come here to dig clams in Samuel and Martha Fitzwilliam's time, and if so, how they had kept their clam baskets afloat, back in those days before inner tubes.

I have no recollection of eating dinner. But I know I went upstairs to bed a little before ten o'clock.

*T*hirteen

❧

I awoke to find bright sunlight slanting onto the bedroom wallpaper, with its huge cabbage roses. Samuel's first wife, Patience, had chosen that paper. I had never met Patience, but I had heard she was well named, a small, plain woman who had never been known to raise her voice against anything or anybody. As I often did, I wondered if it was some secret longing for self-assertion that had led her to choose this flamboyant wallpaper.

I was alone in the fourposter bed. After a moment I remembered. Samuel had said that he planned to ride horseback to East Hampton to conduct some business.

I got out of bed and went to the rear window. Fergus, the young Scotsman who with his wife, Flora, was working out a seven-year bond, was down there in the open space in front of the stable. Red hair bright in the sunlight, he was currying the roan saddle horse, Satin, that I usually rode. The carriage had been drawn out of the stable too. With a cloth in one palsied hand, Hannibal was rubbing its oil lamps. He was older than the two women slaves, perhaps almost eighty. It was amazing how much work he still managed to do.

I stood for a few moments more looking down at the two men, and the old carriage house, with its second story rooms where Fergus and Flora lived, and the two little slave cabins whose roofs Samuel had found so outrageously expensive.

Soon, I noticed, he would have to spend money reroofing that lean-to he'd had built against the carriage house's northern wall. In it, under lock and key, he kept the musket his father had carried during the Revolution, as well as a pair of pistols. Recently perfected by a young man named Samuel Colt, they could fire six bullets without being reloaded. I felt I knew why he had locked the guns away. He had done so after a distant relative in Georgia had written to him about a slave revolt down there. Apparently he feared that Sarah and Callie and Hannibal might rise up some night and murder us in our beds.

Sounds made me whirl around. They came from the room across the hall——my little girl's whimpers and Flora's soothing voice, with its Scottish burr. My heart gave an alarmed leap. I had felt able to interpret all of Charity's cries, the "I'm-hungry" one, the "I-want-to-be-cuddled" one, and the sheer bad-tempered one. This cry was different. It sounded frightened and bewildered.

I flung open one door of the wardrobe and took down my blue dimity dressing gown. As I slipped into it I saw my reflection in the wardrobe's other door. The marks of Samuel's fingers on my throat were still an ugly dark blue. Outside the bedroom I had worn scarves or high collars these past two days, but I had no time for that now. Besides, Flora already knew that sometimes Samuel turned violent toward me.

I crossed the hall, opened the door. Charity was standing up in her crib, dimpled hands grasping its top rail. Flora had bent her head, its luxuriant hair as red as her husband's, close to Charity's dark curls. "Now, lovey," Flora was saying. "Now, my sweetling."

At sight of me my daughter's whimpers turned to wails. Flora straightened up. "Oh, milady!"

Before she emigrated from Scotland, Flora had been a maid

96

in an earl's household. Hence the "milady" habit. I had tried to break her of it, and most of the time she did call me Mrs. Fitzwilliam, but in moments of stress she forgot.

"I was just about to call you, milady. She does seem poorly this morning. As soon as I came in she began fretting. And she wouldn't eat any of the breakfast I brought her."

I looked at the bowl of gruel on the table beside the crib and then lifted my daughter into my arms. Even in my alarm, I was aware of her beauty. The clustered dark curls. The face that, even at the age of fourteen months, gave promise of becoming heart-shaped.

But now the beautiful eyes looked too bright, and her flushed cheeks were warm to my touch. Heart contracting, I thought of typhoid, diphtheria, scarlet fever. Every year in our village the deaths of children under five outnumbered the deaths among all the rest of the population.

I said, "Flora, go tell Fergus to fetch Dr. Gothwaite." Thank heaven he lived less than half a mile away, on upper Main Street. "Tell him to ride Satin over there. That'll be quicker."

Flora left the room. After a few moments I heard the sound of hooves running down the drive. Then Flora returned to the room. I put Charity back in her crib, and the Scotswoman and I sat on either side of it, talking a little now and then, but mostly just watching Charity's flushed face.

Two sets of hooves in the drive now. I realized that Fergus must have tethered the mare behind Dr. Gothwaite's buggy. After a few moments I heard the doctor's footsteps on the stairs. It wasn't until then that I realized I was still in my nightgown and robe. Well, no matter. Dr. Gothwaite had known me quite literally all my life.

He came in carrying his worn black bag, a frock-coated man who was quite thin except for a stomach that strained the buttons of his waistcoat. He took off his tall hat, revealing a bald pate with a fringe of gray hair, greeted Flora and me, and then set to work. He looked down Charity's throat and into her tiny ears. He moved a stethoscope over her back and chest and then, to her howled objection, he prodded her stomach with his fingers.

At last he said, "No scarlet fever, no typhoid, nothing at all serious. Just colic." He put his stethoscope into his bag and brought out a brown bottle. "Give her a teaspoonful of this right away, and another one at five this afternoon." He handed the bottle to Flora. "She ought to be fine this afternoon, if not sooner."

I said, "Oh, thank you, thank you."

"Why is it that people always thank me for a favorable diagnosis? *I* didn't arrange for her to have colic instead of scarlet fever." Then, in a different tone, "Martha, I want to talk to you for a moment, in your room."

Dr. Gothwaite and I crossed the hall to the bedroom Samuel and I shared. When I had closed the door he said, "How did you get those bruises? And don't try to give me some farfetched explanation. Anyone can see those are fingermarks. Samuel's, I suppose."

"He became—very angry—"

"I didn't suppose he had done it out of sheer good humor. Is this sort of thing happening more frequently than in the past?"

I said evasively. "Not really."

"Had he been drinking?"

"Oh, no!" Years ago, long before I knew him, Samuel had been what people called "a periodical"—that is, a man who drank for days at a time with long stretches of sobriety in between. But soon after he joined the Brethren United in Christ he had stood up in meeting and vowed he would never let another drop pass his lips. So far he had kept that vow.

"Do you think it would do any good to have his pastor talk to him?"

"No. He'd just tell the Reverend Morse to mind his own business."

"I thought that maybe with him being quite religious, leading prayers for the whole household every night—"

98

"That's because he wants the servants to obey God's will."

"Which I imagine is synonymous with Samuel's will. Martha, I not only spanked Charity until she drew her first breath, I did the same thing for you. You know that I'm prepared to do anything to help you, at any time."

"You've proved that," I said quietly.

We looked at each other for a long moment. Then he said, "Well, I'd better get down to the wharf. About fifteen men brought scurvy back from the South Pacific with them."

I cried, "Not men on the *Unicorn!*"

"No. Captain Cantrell makes sure that his men eat well enough to avoid scurvy."

I remembered then how Samuel always complained about Jared's insistence that some of the ship's precious cargo space be used for preserved fruits put up by Hampton Harbor housewives. "If it weren't that he makes more money for me than any of my other captains," I had heard Samuel say, "I would lay down the law to him."

Again Dr. Gothwaite and I looked at each other silently for a moment. Then he said, "What's tomorrow? Thursday?"

The pulse leaped in the hollow of my throat. "Yes."

"I've been spending Thursdays at the infirmary. But I'll drop by Friday to see Charity. Not that I expect to find anything wrong with her, but I'll look in. Well, goodbye, Martha."

When the door had closed behind him, I began to dress. Now that I knew Charity was not seriously ill, all I could think of was Jared. Tomorrow afternoon I would be in his arms.

The day was turning hotter, more sultry. From the big wardrobe I took down an old dress of lavender lawn, the coolest garment I owned. From the top drawer of one of the pair of mahogany highboys—the other chest was Samuel's—I took out a wide choker made of crimson moire. Standing in front of the mirrored wardrobe door I put the ribbon around my neck and fastened its hooks and eyes. It looked and felt uncomfortably warm, and its color clashed with my dress, but no matter. It hid those ugly bruises.

I stepped out into the hall, closing the door behind me.

A car passed along Converse Street, its radio tuned so loud that even here, at the back of the house, I could hear Diana Ross singing an old John Lennon number.

I looked down. I was wearing faded blue cotton shorts. The sunburn I had received the day Martin and I went clamming had turned to a light tan, but my legs still looked pale for someone who had been in Hampton Harbor for almost three weeks.

I knew what I would see if I turned around and reopened the door of my room. No fourposter, no fine old wardrobe, no pair of mahogany highboys. Just a bed with a cheap maple head-board and a dressing table with a blue skirt. Over the back of a chair, placed close to the wall with its gray and blue paper, my nightgown would be draped.

And the door across the hall. If I opened it I would see a small room that, summer-house fashion, had been crammed with sleeping accommodations for four people, two bunk beds against one wall, and against another a studio hi-riser that could sleep two.

No worried young Scotswoman. No crib. No beautiful child with glossy dark curls and flushed cheeks.

For a moment, thinking of Charity's warm weight in my arms, I had a sense of loss. Then I realized how absurd it was to feel that. If Charity had existed at all, she must have lived out her life many, many years ago.

I went down the stairs. I wasn't hungry, but I would scramble an egg and toast two bread slices. Martin had said I must eat.

*F*ourteen

❧

The next day was cooler. In such weather, driving to the county offices in Riverhead would not be so onerous. Yet I kept procrastinating. I felt too tired to make the drive, I told myself, knowing that what I really feared was not the drive but what I might discover at the end of it.

I would compromise. I would go to the supermarket. Afterwards, I would visit the shoe store on Main Street in hope of finding a nice pair of sandals. Then, if I felt up to it, I would drive to Riverhead.

I put on white cotton shorts and a green tee shirt. I checked my shoulder bag to be sure I had keys, money, and credit cards. Then I went out the back door—

Red hair bright in the sunlight, Fergus was tightening Satin's saddle girth just outside the stable door. I walked toward him, holding a leather crop in one hand, and raising the black velvet skirt of my riding habit an inch or so above the grass with the other. How I hoped that my manner appeared just as it had on all those other days when I had taken long rides through the wooded hills surrounding the harbor. Samuel approved of those rides. Ever since he had decided that exercise might help me to conceive a son, he had encouraged me to pursue all forms of physical activity, just as long as they did not include visits to my friends. *That* was considered "traipsing."

Fergus straightened up as I approached. "Good day to you, Mrs. Fitzwilliam. A fine day it is, too."

I agreed.

"Flora tells me that the young one got over her colicky spell."

"Yes. You'd never know she'd been sick. I left her and Flora playing pattycake."

"That's good." He gave the mare's shining rump a little slap. "Well, she's ready for you."

He bent, cupped his hands. I put a booted foot on those interlaced fingers, and he boosted me into the side saddle. As the mare carried me down the drive, I called a greeting to Hannibal, who was raking fallen catalpa leaves from the front yard.

I rode several hundred yards down Monroe Street and then turned east through a series of narrow streets toward open country. Quite a few people were out on this fine day. I kept raising my riding crop to greet friends and acquaintances. Mr. Givens, the apothecary, on his white horse that looked almost as gaunt as he did. Ted Dorrance, the banker's son, and his impressively-bosomed mother who rode behind a liveried coachman in an open carriage. Miss Clay, who kept a grammar school. Thanks to the generosity of a cousin of my mother's, my two farm-bred sisters and I had been able to stay in the cousin's house several winters and attend Miss Clay's school. Despite her seventy-odd years, she sat severely erect on the seat of her surrey, reins gathered in her mittened hands. To all of these people I smiled, hoping that they would never guess that my rebellious heart was singing, "Jared! Jared!"

The last of the streets petered out into a track that led through woods of oak and maple and an occasional juniper. It was hot there under the over-arching branches, and I had to keep brushing insects away from my face. When I could, I took another trail that led toward the bay. Soon I was riding along an almost treeless hillside, with the bay on my left. I was scarcely aware of that sparkling blue water, though. My attention was centered on a clump of trees ahead, high on the hillside.

The whinny of a horse. Satin tossed her head and nickered an answer. My heart swelled. I turned onto a barely perceptible path leading upward and touched Satin's neck lightly with the crop. Then I was inside the little copse of trees that surrounded the fort's crumbling stone walls. A gray horse, no doubt hired from the Harbor Livery Stable, stood tethered to a tree. Jared emerged from the ruined and roofless fort. He tied Satin's reins to a sapling. Then I slid from the saddle into his arms.

We kissed. All the pent-up desire of many a long, long month was in that kiss. He took my riding hat from my head. Then, with his arm around me, we stepped through the crumbling doorway.

It was like a little room, floored with grass and buttercups and clover, roofed with only the blue sky. He had spread a dark blue blanket on the ground. Beside it stood a small wicker hamper.

For perhaps a minute we did not speak, just sat on the blanket, lips clinging. Through the velvet of my riding habit I could feel the warmth of his hands.

At last, long fingers on either side of my face, he said, "You are more beautiful than ever, my darling."

"I have someone to stay beautiful for."

He kissed me again. Then his hands were undoing the buttons of my bodice. Eyes closed, I felt desire like a warm, inward melting. Now he was unwinding the white stock from around my throat—

"Martha!" His voice had a sickened sound. "Your throat—"

I opened my eyes. "It doesn't matter. It no longer hurts."

When he answered his voice was quiet. "I'd like to kill him, kill him with my bare hands."

"Oh, please, please!" My need for his love-making was like

103

a torment. "We have so little time. Don't let anything spoil it."

He looked down at me for a long moment, rage in his eyes, face pale under its tan. Then he said, "You are right, my love." His mouth covered mine, and his arms bore me backward onto the blanket.

For an unmeasured interval I had no consciousness of anything except our joined bodies, the fulfillment of the desire that had consumed me so many nights in that Monroe Street house, and which must have tormented Jared as his ship sailed under those southern constellations I had never seen. When that first storm of passion had exhausted itself, we lay quiet for a while, and then again turned to each other.

At last we arranged our dishevelled clothing. Although I had no recollection of it, Jared at some point must have drawn the tortoiseshell pins from my hair. It was hanging loose down my back and the pins were scattered over the blanket. With his help I gathered them up, coiled my hair at the nape of my neck, and thrust the pins into place.

At last Jared said, in a voice that sounded all the firmer for its quietness, "We will talk now."

I tensed, knowing what he was about to say, and knowing with anguish that I must deny him.

"You must leave that— You must leave your husband."

"Jared, I told you the last time you were here—"

He said, as if I hadn't spoken, "Best that you come aboard the night the *Unicorn* is to sail. Don't bring any luggage, even a portmanteau. The only important thing is for you to get safely out of the house. I'll take you ashore in Newport, Virginia. I have cousins who live in a town not far from there. You can stay with them until I get back."

"Jared, I can't! I love you. I've never loved any man but you and never shall. But I can't give up my little girl, not even for you."

"I didn't mean for you to. You can bring her with you."

"I can't do that to my child! If there was any hope of Samuel giving me a divorce it would be different. But he never would.

104

And he would take Charity from me. The law would be on his side, of course."

"But if he couldn't find you—"

"Oh, he'd find me, he'd find me! He's a rich man, far richer than you would think from that modest house of his. He would pay people to find me. He'd pay as much money as it took for as long as it took."

"We could go far away, the three of us. California, say."

"He'd stil find us. And even if he didn't— Oh, Jared! You and I couldn't marry. I couldn't go through some—bigamous ceremony. It would only make things worse for us and for Charity when Samuel found us. And even if by some unbelievable good fortune he didn't find us, think what our lives would be, always waiting for the blow to fall, always wondering, wherever we settled, if our neighbors suspected I was a runaway wife. We'd always be uneasy. Charity would sense that, and become uneasy herself. Oh, Jared! She's such a beautiful, wonderful little girl. She deserves to grow up in a settled world, with friends and neighbors who have always known her parents—"

My voice trailed off. Jared sat silent, head half bowed, hands on his updrawn knees. Finally I said, "Did you bring food in that basket?"

He said, with an obvious effort, "Yes. I had the people at the Main Street Hotel put up a lunch for us."

There were ham sandwiches, hard-boiled eggs, and plums and apples. There was also a bottle of burgundy and two wine glasses.

While we ate we talked, rather stiffly, of various matters, I told him that the previous night Samuel had spoken of how it might be wise to get out of whaling in a few years, before the collapse he could foresee cost him a great deal of money. I asked Jared what he would do if this next voyage of the *Unicorn's* turned out to be its last, and he said he would have no trouble getting some other ship. In fact, two other shipowners had approached him about assuming a command. One owner was in the China trade. The other carried timber and hides and

105

a few passengers to Europe, and brought back everything from fine English furniture to tulip bulbs from Holland.

We returned to the wicker basket the checkered tablecloth, napkins, empty wine bottle, and wine glasses. Then Jared said, "Have you spoken your last word?"

"About leaving Samuel? Yes, Jared."

Unless, I thought, Samuel ever visited his cruelty upon Charity. *Then* I would take her and run away—all by myself, if necessary. But I felt sure he would not maltreat her. He never had, not even when her crying annoyed him. At times he even seemed proud of her, looking pleased when people pointed out that her glossy dark curls were the same shade as his beard, and her eyes the same brown as his.

Jared's voice was bitter. "If that is your last word, then what are we to do? Meet here at intervals of several months or a year or more, and spend the rest of our lives longing for each other?"

"I—I'm afraid so."

Only it would not be for the rest of our lives, I thought sadly. Right now Jared felt he had no choice except to love me. But he was a man, and young, and in robust health. Sooner or later he would rebel against loving a woman he could not really have. And he would meet an attractive young woman in London, or Amsterdam, or Newport News—

And what of me, after he took a wife? Well, I would just go on living with Samuel, and raising my little girl. For my heart's sustenance, I would have to turn to memory.

I said, "Forgive me, my dearest."

"Forgive? It's not your fault. It's just the way things are. If I could, I suppose I might wish your little girl out of existence." Oh, no, Jared, I thought. Don't say that. "But I can't, and so I'll just have to go on as content as possible with having you only once in a while."

We lay down then, hands clasped but otherwise not touching. This was the third time we had met in this place. The first time had been in glorious September, with a few gold and scarlet leaves already showing on the maples around the old

106

fort. The next time had been eleven months later, with a breeze off the bay stirring the langorous August heat.

Our last meeting?

He said, as if his thoughts had paralleled mine, "Will you meet me here again before the *Unicorn* sails? She's in drydock now, you know." I hadn't known. "After that rough passage around the Horn, her seams need caulking. Your husband wants me to be there for every step of the procedure, but just the same, I think I can get away. I'll get word to you somehow. I can always think of some reason to send a note to the owner's house."

"Yes."

I knew I should be going. Samuel usually did not leave his Main Street office until after five. Sometimes, though, he came home earlier.

I said, "I'd better leave now. I'll go first." I wished we could ride together to the outskirts of the village, and thus have those extra minutes. But it would be foolish to run that additional risk of being seen together.

Outside the fort we kissed and embraced for a long moment. When Jared released me I saw that he was so pale under his tan that his skin had taken on a yellowish cast. He helped me into the saddle, untied Satin's reins, handed them to me. I looked down into his taut, beloved face, said, "Goodbye, my darling," and rode off. I didn't look back, not even when I reached the edge of the thick woods.

*F*ifteen

As I guided Satin onto Monroe Street, I heard the clock in the Methodist church tower strike four. A minute or so later I rode up the drive of my house. Fergus came out of the stable to greet me. I took my foot from the stirrup and slid to the ground.

"Nice ride, ma'am?"

"Very nice."

"You were gone a long time."

"I called on several families."

Lies. As a young girl, I had despised liars. But an adulteress, I reflected, has little choice except to become a liar also.

Fergus led Satin into the stable.

As I walked toward the rear entrance of the house, I looked up. Flora stood at the nursery window, with Charity in her arms. Flora smiled, and Charity gave a gurgling laugh and waved to me.

I opened the door.

The refrigerator gave a preliminary rumble, then settled down to a steady hum.

Dizziness engulfed me. I grasped the back of one of the

kitchen's two steel tubing chairs and managed to lower myself to its plastic seat. I had my straw handbag in my hand. Automatically I placed it on the kitchen table.

My dizziness had lessened. I looked down. I still wore the white cotton shorts and green tee shirt I remembered putting on that morning. Then, with my car keys in my handbag, I had walked out the back door and into—

Where in God's name had I been?

While Martha Fitzwilliam had lain in her lover's arms, what had *I* been doing? I, Gail Loring, late of the advertising firm of Horton and Jedlow, and even later of the Morse-Whitlow Clinic.

Where had I been all those hours? Walking about the streets? Staring through my parked car's windshield at waves washing up on a beach? Shopping? If I went out that back door now, would I find my car standing in the drive, its hood still warm and with groceries in its trunk?

Only one thing I felt sure of. Being this sure might make others conclude that I was crazy indeed, but nevertheless I was now convinced that Martha and Jared had really existed. Those hours up at the old fort had seemed too real to be anything but the reliving of an actual event. Seated on that ugly kitchen chair, I could recall everything about Jared Cantrell. His sun-browned face with the squint lines at the corners of the eyes. His strong, long-fingered hands, with the hairs on his wrists glinting gold in the sunlight. The feel of his warm mouth on mine. The mixture of pain and near-rage in his voice as he pleaded with me to leave Samuel.

Not only had those two lived, but the others also—Samuel, and Charity, and Fergus and Flora, and Hannibal and Sara and Callie. And they *must* have left some sort of official records somewhere, even though they had lived long before birth certificates, social security numbers, drivers' licenses, and all those other means by which officialdom keeps track of us from our first breath onward. Yes, even though neither of the cemeteries or the village clerk's office had yielded me any information, surely I would find records somewhere.

I looked at my watch. Almost four-thirty. Far too late to drive to Riverhead. The county offices would be closed by the time I got there. But I would go tomorrow, no matter how I felt.

I forced myself to my feet, opened the door, and stepped out into the backyard, a yard that ran north and south, not east and west, like the one I had walked across only minutes ago. And no stable here, no little slave cabins. Just that collapsing tool shed and, in the driveway, my rented car.

Yes, I had been shopping. Two grocery-filled bags stood in the trunk. Evidently I had been at the supermarket not too long ago, because when I felt a milk carton I found it still cold. I looked inside the car. A shoe box lay on the seat next to the driver's. I opened it. Flat-heeled leather sandals, the same ones I had seen in a shop window my first day in Hampton Harbor. Why I had left my purchases in the car after I parked it here in the drive, I would never know.

I placed the shoe box atop the groceries in one bag and carried both bags into the house.

Sixteen

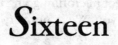

Rain was falling when I awoke the next morning. From the look and sound of it, it was no passing summer shower. The rain fell from a solid gray overcast sky with a persistence that suggested November rather than July. The temperature was cool, too, probably somewhere in the low sixties. As I dressed in white duck pants and a pink cotton turtleneck, I reflected that the weather would make driving harder. On the other hand, it would cut down on traffic.

A little after eleven I mounted the steps of the Criminal Courts Building in Riverhead and, directed by a uniformed guard, found a door labeled "District Attorney for Suffolk County." Beyond it was a large room illuminated by a harsh fluorescent glare that mingled with the gray light coming through the windows. A long counter stretched halfway across the room. Beyond the counter a half dozen clerks sat at desks, some leafing through papers, others punching computers. At the rear of the room was a door marked "District Attorney, Private." Along one wall hung a row of large framed photographs, probably of former district attorneys.

I approached the counter. A plump blonde girl got up from her desk and walked toward me. "Help you?"

"Yes, thank you. I wonder if I could look up a case in your back files."

"No problem. We got microfilm going back years and years. I could look it up for you. We're not very busy just now. What name?"

"Samuel Fitzwilliam."

"Spelling?"

I spelled the last name for her.

"Okay. Now what year?"

"Around eighteen-forty. Or maybe you'll find it a year or so before or after that."

"Eighteen-*forty!*" One would have thought I had named a year predating the Flood.

I said, disconcerted, "You told me your files went far back."

"They do. Nineteen-thirty-one." Her tone was defensive. "That was a long time ago."

"What happened to the files of cases before nineteen-thirty-one?"

"How should I——I mean, all I know is we don't keep them here. Maybe some were sent to the archives up in Albany. Maybe some were shredded. This department can't house every scrap of paper, just on the chance that once in a blue moon somebody's going to ask about something that happened more than a hundred years ago."

"I suppose not." So it had been for nothing, that journey over crowded, rain-slippery roads. "Well, thank you."

As I started to turn away, the row of photographs on the wall again caught my eye. "Are those photographs of former district attorneys?"

"They sure are. Photos of every D.A. since this was named the county seat, only the first few aren't photos. They're what-do-you-call-'ems, etchings. See that one over there? He was elected in eighteen-thirty-eight. If your Samuel What's-his-name was mixed up in some sort of trial back then, that was probably the D.A. who prosecuted the case." She sounded as if she felt that her department had redeemed itself as a preserver of the past.

Filled with vague new hope, I walked over to the framed etching she had pointed out. A man with a large head and impressive gray muttonchop whiskers looked at me sternly across the gap of a century and a half. Beneath the frame a brass plate red: "Benjamin Gotobed, 1838–1848." So he must have served more than one term.

With that faint hope quickening, I thought, what a strange name. And lucky for my purposes that it was. A name like Smith or Baker wouldn't have helped me at all.

I turned around to find that the blonde still stood at the counter, watching me. I walked back to her and said, "This Benjamin Gotobed—"

"Got-o-bed. It has nothing to do with going to bed." I felt she had hoped she would get a chance to correct my pronunciation. "When I first came here somebody told me the name was Danish, or Norwegian, or some language like that, and it means Obey God."

"That's interesting. Do you know if there are any people of that name around here now?"

She shrugged. "Seems to me I've seen the name in the phone book, but I'm not sure. You could look it up."

"I will. Well, thank you very much."

"No problem."

There was a phone booth out in the hall. I went inside it and opened the local phone directory. Two Gotobeds were listed, a Howard Gotobed on Rondel Street and a Paul Gotobed on Macklin Street.

I left the booth and consulted the guard, who told me how to reach both addresses. I decided to try Howard Gotobed first, since his house was only a few blocks away.

The house, set back on a lawn that needed mowing, was a small frame bungalow whose white paint had grown dingy. I went up the walk and knocked on the door.

It opened a few inches. A small wrinkled face haloed by white curls peered out at me. "Yes?"

I sensed that her abruptness was caused not by bad manners, but timidity. I said, "May I speak to Mr. Howard Gotobed?" I remembered to use the correct pronunciation.

"He's asleep right now. Who wants him?"

"My name is Gail Loring. I'm trying to find out about a—a trial that probably took place around 1840. I've learned that the district attorney then was a Mr. Benjamin Gotobed. If Mr. Howard Gotobed is a descendant, he might possibly be able to help me—"

My voice trailed off. The little woman's eyes, faded blue behind rimless glasses, searched my face. "This is something important to you, isn't it?"

"Very."

She seemed to make up her mind about me. "Howard Gotobed was my husband. He passed away fifteen years ago." Still speaking, she opened the door wider. "I left the phone in his name. Safer that way. Some people might rob you if they think you're a woman alone. Or they might call up and say nasty things, you know how it is."

"Yes, I know."

"Come in. I may be able to help you."

The door opened directly into the living room. It was a scrupulously clean room; I felt sure that the floral carpet's threadbare state, and the worn places on the arms of the maroon upholstered sofa and easy chair, were the result not of willful neglect but lack of money.

I sat in the upholstered chair. She sat on the sofa, thin, big-knuckled hands clasped in the lap of her cotton print dress. I wondered how much she weighed. Probably no more than the average ten-year-old.

She said, "He was Howard's ancestor, not mine, of course. But I got to know a lot about him. Howard set great store by the district attorney, his picture being in the Criminal Courts Building and all. In a way, our not having children made old

114

Benjamin seem all the more important to Howard, if you see what I mean."

I felt I did. Howard had had no children—nor much else, to judge by this room—and so an ancestor, however remote, who had held public office was important to his esteem.

"Howard inherited old Benjamin's diaries."

My pulses quickened. "Diaries?"

"Yes. Howard had them bound in leather. Cost more than we could afford, really. That's them over there."

Across the room stood a small two-shelf bookcase. It held a Bible, volume after volume of *Reader's Digest Condensed Books,* and two fat volumes encased in leather.

"Howard wanted to have them printed, but there was never enough money for that, so he just had them bound. Fortunately old Benjamin had a good clear handwriting, even though the ink faded to that funny brown color. Howard used to read and reread the diaries. Sometimes he even read them aloud to me. Sometimes I dipped into them myself."

I leaned forward. "Did those diaries ever mention a Samuel Fitzwilliam?"

She frowned, concentrating. "Hampton Harbor man?"

My heart began to race. "That's the one."

"And you say you think this trial you want to know about took place in 1840?"

"Around there, if there was such a trial."

"I'll look in the diaries. For some reason, that name Fitzwilliam sticks in my memory. I think it's in the second volume. Yes, if it was in 1840, it would be."

She went over to the bookcase, came back with one of the bound volumes, and sat with the book opened on her lap. As she bent over it, turning the pages, I could see her pink scalp through the white curls.

"Here it is. It's dated July 18, 1840. You want me to read it to you?"

"Please." Half in hope, half in terror, I realized that I might be about to learn the nature of my forebear's crime.

She read, "This whole end of Long Island is in an uproar over the Samuel Fitzwilliam case. People in Hampton Harbor are calling him the Monster of Monroe Street. How I wish he could be brought to trial, with me as his prosecutor! It is not just that it would be enormously satisfying to convict the perpetrator of such an atrocity. There is also the benefit that would accrue to my career. A trial like that, lasting for many months, would make my name known throughout the state. The governorship surely would be within my reach. But since there is to be no trial, the sensation surrounding the matter will soon become stale news. In a few decades, even Hampton Harbor people will remember him only vaguely, if at all. In a few scores of years, not even his descendants will be acquainted with his story in any detail."

His descendants. As one of Samuel Fitzwilliam's descendants, I knew Benjamin Gotobed's prophecy to have been true.

Mrs. Gotobed was looking at me. "That's all," she said.

I cried, "Are you sure?"

"Yes. The next item is about the Grand Jury. It was meeting to decide something or other about a bribery scandal. You know, I realize now why I remembered that paragraph about Samuel Fitzwilliam. It was because it also mentions old Benjamin's wanting to be governor. It's the only place in the diaries that he gives himself away like that. But I guess he was a disappointed man, just like—"

She broke off. She must have seen then some of the disappointment I felt, because she said, "You want to see the diary for yourself?"

"Yes, please."

She extended it to me. "Don't worry about handling it. Their ink wasn't much good in those days, but they made their paper to last."

The paragraph, written in a fine copperplate hand, was just as she had read it to me. I knew no more than before about the nature of Samuel Fitzwilliam's crime, but at least I was sure now that there had *been* a crime.

116

I said, "There's another Gotobed listed in the Riverhead phone book. Do you think that he—"

"That's my husband's younger brother. Paul wouldn't be able to tell you anything. He never took any interest in old Benjamin. After Howard passed on, I felt Paul ought to have the diaries, but he didn't want them."

I handed the volume back to her. "Thank you very much indeed for letting me see this."

"You're not going!"

"Yes. There's a lot of bad traffic between here and Hampton Harbor, and the rain doesn't help."

"All the more reason why you should stay for a nice cup of tea. This is just the sort of day for it."

I saw that she was more than old and poor and afraid. She was lonely.

"Well, thank you. I think I could do with some tea before I start back."

She brought me fragrant jasmine tea, served in what I am sure was her last bone china cup. The one from which she drank her own tea was of thick white crockery. We also had some rather stale ginger cookies. I could tell that she very much wanted to know why I was so interested in something that had happened generations ago in a small Long Island village. But she was too polite to ask me, and so instead she talked of a trip to Yellowstone she and her husband had made twenty-five years ago.

Finally I was able to leave. At the door she said, "If there is any other way I can help you, let me know, will you?"

"I certainly will. And again, thank you."

Seventeen

🙠

As I drove back to the Harbor, with rain slashing against the windshield almost faster than the wheezing blade could wipe it away, I reflected that not only had I learned that Samuel Fitzwilliam had indeed committed some monstrous crime, I also had learned that, to avoid trial, he must have fled the village afterward. Hence no Fitzwilliam grave in either of the local cemeteries. Had he taken his young wife and his child with him? Apparently, since there was no headstone in the cemeteries for them, either.

Where had he taken them? Where had they lived out the rest of their lives?

It suddenly occurred to me that I might find a clue to the answer if I worked backward through the generations, starting with myself.

Not only I but my mother and my grandmother and my grandmother's sister, Great Aunt Louise, had been born in Manhattan. Their parents, my great-grandparents, had grown up in Brooklyn. That was as far back as I knew, although my impression was that my great-great-grandparents also had been Brooklynites from birth.

118

But Great Aunt Louise was still alive, down in her Florida condominium. Surely her knowledge of family history should extend back at least fifty years farther than mine. Thus she should have some knowledge of ancestors who had lived on a generation or two after Samuel Fitzwilliam had fled from the law.

Since she had left New York, I had kept my contacts with Aunt Louise to a minimum. A phone call at Christmas, and that was about it. But now I resolved to call her that very evening.

As I approached my rented house I saw, with a blend of surprised pleasure and apprehension, that Martin's car stood at the curb. I turned into the drive. He got out of his car, wearing in dark slacks and a Madras sport coat. We met at the front door.

I said, "I didn't think you'd be back for another four days."

"A friend of mine said he'd take detailed notes on all the lectures I'll be missing."

Fitting the key into the lock I said, "And that will be all right with the college?"

"I think so." I could tell he meant he hoped so.

We went into the front hall and then into the little parlor. As we sat down on the worn, overstuffed sofa, I had a memory of Jared Cantrell in this room, one elbow propped on the marble fireplace mantel, hazel eyes bright in his sun-browned face.

Martin said, "All right. Tell me. Is it the same as when I left?"

I felt too tired and discouraged to try to evade him. "You mean, do I sometimes find myself reliving the life of another woman, a woman who lived in this house more than a hundred and fifty years ago? Yes, I do."

I paused, but when he just looked at me, gray eyes worried behind his glasses, I said, "Martha Fitzwilliam was in love with someone. He was the captain of one of her husband's whaleships."

My words sounded absurd to my own ears. For a bleak moment I saw myself as he or anyone else probably would see me—a mentally unstable woman, weaving elaborate hallucina-

119

tions out of something a drunken great-aunt had once said. Then I reminded myself that now I had objective evidence that someone named Samuel Fitzwilliam had perpetrated a monstrous act in this village a century and a half ago. The diary of a contemporary county official confirmed it. And information that Bert Jeffers had supplied seemed to indicate that this was the house in which it had happened. Surely no more than one house had been moved from Monroe Street to Converse Street in April of 1892, the month and year set down in that old ledger.

I had no intention of telling Martin any of the details of Martha Fitzwilliam's affair with Jared Cantrell. Fortunately, he did not ask for them. Instead he said, "I came back here because I had to. How the hell could I concentrate on the Modern Deconstructionists when I was worrying about you?" His voice became pleading. "Won't you get out of this house? I don't know what to make of the things you've told me. But whether those things really happened or just—happened in your mind, they haven't been good for you. You look as if you've lost another pound or so."

He leaned toward me. "I'm afraid of what may happen to you if you stay in this house."

I too was afraid. Desperately as I wanted to know what had once happened here, I was terrified at the thought that I might find myself reliving an episode that, a century-and-a-half later, still echoed in my own life. But I felt I had no choice.

I said, "I can't turn back now. I think that if I tried to, if I left this house right now and returned to New York, I really would break down. It's—it's as if this house has something to tell me something I must know before I go on with my life. And so I have to wait—"

My voice trailed off. He said nothing, just looked at me with baffled eyes.

After a moment I said, "Is there an old Revolutionary fort here, overlooking the bay?"

"There once was. The British built it, out near Cedar Point.

There's not much of it left now, just a few stones within a grove of trees." He paused. "Why do you ask?"

"I'm just curious. I heard someone mention an old fort, and I thought I might drive out there and look at it."

I could tell he thought there was more to it than that, but he didn't challenge me. "I'd better get back to the office," he said heavily, "and see what's happened. I didn't stop there, just came straight here. But first——"

He reached inside his Madras jacket, brought out a business card, then a pen. "This has the office phone number, and I'll write down my apartment phone." He rose and placed the card on the fireplace mantel. "Don't lose this. And call me at any time, day or night."

I too stood up. "Martin, I'm so sorry." Sorry, I meant, not to do as he urged. "I——I can't understand why you bother with me. I've told you about my background. And I've given you evidence that I might be——off my rocker. And yet you——" My voice trailed off.

His smile was wry. "I don't know why either. I just know that what happens to you matters to me. It matters a lot. I've found that out these last few days, trying to concentrate on lectures and worrying about you instead."

He put his arms around me and kissed me, a long kiss, fervent and yet gentle. When he lifted his head I still clung to him, cheek pressed against his shoulder. I wanted to say, "I love you. Take me with you, right now." But for his sake, as well as my own, I couldn't say that. I had to see it through, this strange journey that all unknowingly I had embarked upon the day I approached this plain, rundown, and yet——to me——strangely welcoming house.

I stepped back, tried to smile. "Goodbye for now, Martin."

"Goodbye. And remember, call me if you need me."

I nodded, wondering if he would call *me,* whether or not I called him.

When he had gone, the house seemed oppressively silent,

even though I again had the sense that underneath the silence other lives were moving through their own time—

I felt an urgent need to get outdoors. I would drive to that old fort, I decided, rain or no rain. The problem was that Martha Fitzwilliam had gone there—or at least in my fantasy had seemed to go there—on horseback, following trails through the woods. Even if the trails still existed, they would do me little good.

Probably, I reflected, some sort of road ran fairly close to the fort now. The thing to do was to go to that Main Street shop two doors from Martin's real estate agency and get a copy of the points-of-interest map I had seen in its window. The trouble with that was that I would be risking an awkward encounter with Martin.

Miss Blaisdell. She had spent eighty-odd years here, and so surely she could direct me. I looked up her number and dialed.

"That old fort?" she said. "The one the British built to take potshots at Yankee ships in the sound? It's nothing but a bunch of rocks now. Why would you want to go look at it?"

"I've always been interested in things like that," I said feebly.

"Well, at least I hope you're not going there in the rain."

I held onto my temper. "It seems to be slackening off now, or maybe I'll wait until tomorrow. But anyway, if you could tell me how to get there—"

"Well, follow One-fourteen about a couple of miles to Widow Haskell's Path, turn left—" She went on, while I scribbled her directions on an old envelope I had found in my handbag.

Perhaps two minutes later she concluded, "Make a left turn, then a right. After about a hundred yards you'll see a marker on the right side of the road, pointing up a footpath. The marker says something like, 'Ruins of British Fort Built in 1778.' Follow the footpath—it's only about a quarter-mile long—and you're there."

"Thank you very much, Miss Blaisdell. Well, I'll say good—"

"I saw Martin Crowley waiting outside your house until you drove up."

"Yes," I said noncommittally.

"Didn't stay long, did he?"

"He—he had business to attend to."

From all I hear, he's a fine young man. A really good catch. Girl would be a fool to pass up a chance like him."

"I suppose you're right." Too late, I realized I should have told her he'd come here only to discuss a fine point in the lease. "Well, goodbye," I hung up quickly, picked up my shoulder bag, and headed toward the door.

Less than an hour later I parked my car at the roadside just beyond a bronze marker with a pointing arrow. The rain had finally stopped, but the trees bordering the fairly steep path still dripped with moisture. It was hot there under the intertwined branches. I was glad when I came out onto a grassy plateau, with the gray waters of the bay on my left. Now I saw, with a leap of my pulses, that the path led to a grove of trees. The grove appeared larger than the one I recalled, but it seemed to me it was still recognizable.

I followed the path into the trees. There it was: the ruined fort. The passage of a century-and-a-half had changed it. The crumbling walls which once had been high enough to give Martha Fitzwilliam and Jared Cantrell at least an illusion of privacy had collapsed almost completely now. But the fallen stones still formed a rectangular pattern.

As I stood there I wondered why I had a sense of triumph. Then the answer came to me. Here was the first recognizable artifact linking my experience in time unmistakably with Martha Fitzwilliam's. True, the floor plan of my rented house seemed to be the same as that of the house where Martha moved, with sweeping skirts, from room to room. But probably hundreds of houses on eastern Long Island built around the turn of the nineteenth century had that floorplan. And nothing else was similar. The Fitzwilliams' heavy mahogany furniture bore no relation to the plastic-and-steel-tubing chairs and battered overstuffed sofas that now filled those rooms. And all the fireplaces were gone, except for the non-working ones in the twin parlors.

But here, it seemed to me, was objective evidence that indeed I had somehow relived an earlier time. The dimensions of the fort were the same as when Martha had met her lover here a century-and-a-half ago. The trees surrounding it were more numerous now, but still the same mixture of oaks, maples, and an occasional juniper.

I walked down the slope that once must have been the line-of-sight for gunners firing at Yankee ships making for Hampton Harbor. Probably in those days there had been no trees left standing along this slope. Even in Martha and Jared's time, tree growth along the line-of-sight had been sparse. Now, though, trees seemed to grow almost as thickly here as on the other three sides of the fort.

I moved to the edge of the bluff riding above the water. There was a rift in the clouds along the western horizon now, so that the declining sun shone as if from beneath a dark, partially raised curtain. It gave golden glints to the satiny gray water. I took off my raincoat, spread it on the drenched grass, and sat down.

A small cabin cruiser down there was moving on a westerly course, the sound of its engine faintly audible. To judge by its slow progress, it was bucking a tide. Time and tide, I thought. Maybe time was not only like a river, as people often said, but also like that bay down there, swept by tides that made it ever changing and yet always the same. Time after time, tide after tide—

Life after life?

With a start I realized that the water below me had become streaked with sunset colors. I looked at my watch. Almost eight. I had best call Aunt Louise the moment I got back to the house.

*E*ighteen

✤

"Hello?" Aunt Louise said. "Hello?" Perhaps the crackling on the line bothered her, or perhaps her deafness had increased since the last time we talked on the phone. But as nearly as I could tell with this bad connection, she was not drunk. Maybe for some reason she had given up alcohol.

I said, for the second time, "It's Gail. How are you, Aunt Louise?"

The crackling noise had stopped. "Oh! Gail." The flatness of her tone told me that she had come to like me no better than she ever had. "Where are you?"

"Out on Long Island. Hampton Harbor."

"Hampton Harbor! What are you doing out there?"

"I rented a house here for the summer. Aunt Louise, do you remember telling me about a Samuel Fitzwilliam who once lived in Hampton Harbor?"

"I do." Obviously she not only remembered telling me; she remembered, and still resented, the way my mother had stormed out onto the porch to check her recital of my grim family heritage.

"As I recall, you didn't know just how many generations there'd been between Samuel Fitzwilliam and you, or mother and me."

"That's right. But would you mind telling me why you're suddenly so interested in—"

"Just curious, that's all. I thought that maybe we could approach it from the other end, moving backward from me, I mean." I went on quickly, before she could interrupt, "Now, I was born in Manhattan, and so was my mother, but you and my grandmother were born in Brooklyn."

"That's right. So were both our parents."

"I thought that was the case. But how about your grandparents?"

"One pair was from Germany. The other pair came from Virginia. Even though they both died while I was still a child, I remember that they spoke with a Southern accent. Their name was Bryce. Oh, another thing. My grandmother told me that *her* father fought for the Confederacy, so I suppose he was a Virginian, too. But I never knew his name, or if I did know I forgot."

My heart was beating hard. The Civil War. The Civil War started only a little more than twenty years after Samuel Fitzwilliam's crime. Now it seemed to me likely that he had fled to Virginia, taking his wife and small daughter with him. Perhaps the Confederate soldier Aunt Louise had just mentioned had been the husband of the grown-up Charity. Or perhaps he had been an adult son of Samuel and Martha Fitzwilliam, the son Samuel had wanted for so long.

The mention of Virginia had reminded me of something else. Jared Cantrell had pleaded with Martha to let him take her on the *Unicorn* down to relatives of his in Virginia. Well, the coincidence was far from surprising. Even back then, Virginia had been not only a large state but a quite populous one. It was easy to believe that the state to which Fitzwilliam had fled was also the one where relatives of Jared Cantrell had lived.

"Aunt Louise, how much do you know about Samuel Fitzwilliam?"

126

"Only what I'd told you that afternoon your mother got so mad at me. He did something terrible, so terrible that people called him a monster. But what he did, and what happened to him because of it, I never knew."

"Who told you what you do know about him?"

"My mother. She found out I'd been spending my Sunday School nickel each week on candy, so she told me that if I kept on like that people would say I was the same as an ancestor of mine who once lived out on Long Island in a place called Hampton Harbor. He lived on Monroe Street, she said, and he did something so wicked that people called him the Monster of Monroe Street."

So perhaps that was how the story had been passed down. Back in the pre-Spock days, parents had used garbled or fragmented legends to frighten children into obedience.

She said, "You haven't told me yet why you're suddenly so interested in all this."

"Yes, I did. I said I just became curious, being out here for the summer and all."

She gave up. "How's Victor?"

I regretted the impulse that had led me, during my last phone conversation with her, to say that I was in love, and expected to marry.

"I don't know how he is. We've stopped seeing each other."

"I figured you had. I mean, it sounded like you were out there on Long Island all alone. Well, I could have predicted as much. Men don't like cold, bossy women."

So she had not forgiven me for telling her, after my mother's death, that she could not live with me in my new apartment. Well, there was no point in arguing with her.

"How is everything going, Aunt Louise?"

"Okay. The cockroaches down here fly and are as big as sparrows, and I don't get along with most of the people in this condominium, but I suppose it could be worse."

"I'm sorry you don't have agreeable neighbors. Well, thank you, Aunt Louise, and goodnight."

127

I hung up quickly. Then, hand still on the phone, I looked down the hallway, dimly illuminated by the day's last glow filtering through the door's fanlight. Feeling a stir of hunger, I realized I'd had no lunch that day. I would cook one of those fast-food dinners I had placed in the refrigerator. I walked down the hall and opened the kitchen door.

I met firelight and lamp glow and the sweet, spicy smell of peach preserves.

Nineteen

❧

Sara stood, back turned to me, at the tin-covered sinkboard, ladling peach preserves into cream-colored earthenware crocks.

"Sara! Why are you still working? Don't you know it's almost nine?"

"Couldn't let them peaches go bad, Miz Martha. The master sure wouldn't like that."

No, Samuel wouldn't like that. Several days before he had arranged to have a farmer deliver, at a bargain rate, a cartload of early peaches to this house. As often happened, I wondered at my husband's strange blend of extravagance and stinginess. Here he was building a Main Street mansion that would outshine the others on Captains' Row. And yet in order to save a dollar or two, he had overwhelmed his aging domestics with all that fruit.

" 'Sides," she said, "I had Callie to help me. She was so tuckered out I told her to go to bed maybe half an hour ago. Anyway, I'm 'bout finished."

She hesitated, looking at me sidewise, her eyes young and

alert in her seamed, dark face. "I was 'gwine wait till tomorrow to give you this, but now you're here—"

Her hand plunged into the pocket of her blue cotton apron, came up with a folded piece of paper. "A boy brought this. Guve it to Hannibal, and he guve it to me."

Heart pounding, I took the note. I knew who it was from. Only one person would need to communicate with me in this roundabout fashion.

Jared had written, without salutation or signature, "I can get away Friday from noon on."

Despair was a bitter taste in my mouth. I could not meet him. Samuel had told me that on Friday the representatives of several New Haven, Connecticut, manufacturers would be here. I was to hold myself in readiness to look at catalogues and help him select wallpapers, carpeting, and some of the furniture for our future Main Street home.

I dared not try to get word to Jared. And so, just as he had the last time his ship was in the Harbor, he would wait for me at the fort until the light began to fade.

And the next day, Saturday, the *Unicorn* was scheduled to sail on the near midnight tide, to be gone—how long? Six months? A year? Two years? However long it would take to fill its holds.

Of course, some ships did not return at all.

I felt that I was suffocating with my need for him, my rebellion against circumstances that kept us wasting our years, our lives, apart from each other. I walked over to the fireplace, dropped the note onto the coals, watched it curl and blacken and then spiral up the chimney. That too was bitter. How I longed to keep that note, hide it away somewhere. Those few written words, that paper his long-fingered hands had touched, might be all I would have of him from now on. And yet I dared not keep it.

I turned around to find Sara watching me. I knew that neither she nor the other two slaves could read. And yet I was sure she

130

knew who had sent the note, and, at least roughly, what it had said, and why I was in such despair now.

She said, "Miz Martha, us got trouble."

I realized she was trying to distract me. "What's that?"

She gestured toward a row of filled crocks lined up to the pine table. "Cellar's full. Where I gwine put all that?"

With an effort, I considered. "There's that closet under the stairs."

"It's pretty full. All those empty boxes."

She meant hat boxes. That was another of Samuel's almost inexplicable economies. Once years ago he had read somewhere that hat boxes could cost as much as a quarter of a dollar each to manufacture. Since then he had insisted that all such boxes be saved because they were "quite valuable." On the floor of the closet under the stairs were neat stacks of boxes that had once held hats—hats belonging to his first wife, and himself, and me, and even baby bonnets people had sent to Charity.

"I think there's a shelf that can be cleared off. Let's go see."

With Sara carrying the lamp, we crossed the hall. I lifted the latch of the door to the cupboard set under the stairs, pulled the door back. Lamplight fell on the head-high stacks of boxes filling one end of the closet, and on an old trunk and two portmanteaus made of brown carpeting, and a shelf filled with stacked newspapers.

"If you put those old papers on the floor, there'll be room on the shelf for the preserves. But for heaven's sake don't do it tonight. Wait until morning."

We closed the door, making sure that the latchstring remained hanging on the inside. One sweltering day years ago, when Callie was alone in the house, she for some reason had gone into the stair closet, unaware that the latchstring had been left hanging on the outside. A gust of wind sweeping down the hall from the kitchen's screened door had slammed the closet door shut. Callie had remained imprisoned until her sister, out in the garden, had finally heard her cries.

131

Sara and I went back into the kitchen. She said, "You come down here for somethin', Miz Martha?"

Because of Jared's note, I'd almost forgotten. "A cup of tea. Mr. Samuel's stomach is a little upset, and he thinks tea might help."

"Take me only a minute."

"No! You finish filling those jars and then go to bed." I reached into the fireplace and lifted the kettle off the hob. "I'll make the tea and carry it up to him."

A few minutes later, teacup in hand, I said goodnight to Sara and stepped out into the hall, closing the door behind me.

Only the faintest glow came through the fanlight now, but it was enough. Enough to show me that there was no latched door in the slanting wooden wall that enclosed the area under the stairs. At some time during all the years since Martha and Sara had peered into that closet, it had been blanked off.

I stood there. My right hand, the one that only a moment ago had held a cup filled with tea, hung empty at my side.

I no longer felt the hunger that had sent me into the kitchen. But I would eat, I told myself grimly. If I were to stay in this house, I would have to keep up my strength.

I turned and went back into the kitchen.

No mingled lamplight and fireglow. No smell of spiced fruit. Only the dull gleam of porcelain and stainless steel.

I switched on the dangling light. I set the oven to 350 degrees. Then I took from the refrigerator a flat box containing a Mrs. Paul's Fishstick Dinner.

I made a lettuce and tomato salad while the fishsticks baked. Then, with the food before me, I sat at the enamel-topped table which occupied, almost exactly, the space where the crock-laden pine table had stood. Although still not really hungry, I finished my meal, rinsed and stacked my dishes. Then I turned out the light and went out into the hall.

Now only the glow from the streetlamp outside came through the fanlight, but it was strong enough that I could see the slanting wall that concealed the understairs area. An un-

132

broken wall now. But only about half an hour ago, it seemed to me, I had lifted a latch and opened a door, and a black slave and I had looked into a closet.

That closet. That closet was involved in something terrible. And no matter that it had happened generations ago. It would happen again. And to me.

I don't know why, after my lonely but uneventful meal, sudden terror should descend upon me, but it did. A voice in my mind began to say, "Get out! Get out while you still can."

They had vanished, those resolutions of mine to stay in this house no matter what. With my blood drumming in my ears, I ran to the front of the hall, up the stairs. I flipped light switches, first in the upper hall, then in my bedroom.

From the closet I hauled out my suitcase, put it on the bed, opened it. I would go to a motel tonight. Would I call Martin tonight or in the morning? That was something I would decide later. Right now all I wanted was to get away, away from this place where present time now seemed like the rotten flooring of some abandoned mine, ready to crumble at any moment and send me plunging into God-only-knew-what hideousness in the darkness below.

I packed, jerking open dresser drawers, sliding garments off hangers. I closed my suitcase. What else to take? My handbag, my sketching case, and the tennis racquet I hadn't used because I'd had no one to play with. I couldn't manage all those things at once. Best to take my suitcase down to the car now, and then come back for the racquet and sketching case. As for my sheets and blankets, and my variety-store dishes and knives and forks, I might pick them up tomorrow, or just leave them here.

My very preparations for flight seemed to have increased my panic. Aware of cold sweat on my forehead and running down my sides under my white cotton blouse, I carried my suitcase into the hall and started down the stairs.

Someone down there. Someone standing tall and dark against the wall at the foot of the stairs, ready to bar my escape through the front door.

My heart gave a sickened leap. In blind panic I started to turn to retreat up the stairs. Somehow I lost my balance, dropped the suitcase, fell onto my side. Then I was sliding down the stairs. My frantically reaching hand wrapped itself around one of the banister's spindles, checking my descent. I managed to turn over and place my palms on a step. Reaching up to grasp the banister railing, I struggled to my feet. Then my legs gave under me, and I sank onto the step.

Still something down there. A shadow. *My* shadow, the shadow of my seated self, stretching along the floor and a little way up the wall, although not as far up as when I had stood erect. Quite literally, I had been frightened by my own shadow.

And in my senseless panic, I might have broken my neck.

From now on I would try to ignore that drumbeat of alarm which, even now, seemed to throb deep in my mind. I would keep the resolution I had made both to myself and to Martin. I would stay here, because I could not face the rest of my life not knowing what he had done in this house, that man whose blood moved through my veins.

I stood up. Apparently I had not hurt myself much, although I was sure I would awaken tomorrow with bruises and sore muscles. My suitcase had burst open, strewing bras and panties and sweaters and skirts halfway down the stairs. I placed my suitcase on the floor. Then, somewhat unpleasantly aware of my shadow-self mimicking my motions, I retrieved my belongings. I carried my refilled suitcase into the bedroom.

*T*wenty

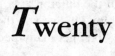

Sunlight on my closed eyelids awoke me. Immediately I remembered my graceless panic of the night before—my body
sprawled on the stairs and my suitcase spilling its contents. I
recalled, too, the resolve I had made before I fell asleep. Surely
somewhere there was a record of what had happened in this
house a century-and-a-half ago. If it were humanly possible, I
was going to find it.

There was a whaling museum on Main Street, a large white
structure that looked like an uneasy cross between Monticello
and the First National Bank. Surely it would have at least some
record of the *Unicorn*.

I got out of bed and began to dress.

Less than an hour later I walked up the museum's brick path
between a ship's longboat and a large try pot, each hung inside
a white wooden framework. I opened one half of a tall screen
door and stepped inside a wide hallway with a gleaming hard-
wood floor. In a room to my left a tall, dignified-looking man
of about fifty stood before a fireplace, studying a framed canvas
that hung above the black marble mantelpiece. From the way

his head was tipped at an angle, I judged he was trying to decide whether or not the picture had been hung properly.

As I stepped over the threshold, he turned and smiled at me. We exchanged good mornings. Then I asked, "Could you tell me where I could find the curator?"

"You're looking at him. I'll give you the VIP tour if you like. Nice day like this, we don't get many people. Everybody goes to the beach."

"Thank you. I'd love to take you up on that. But right now I'm looking for some specific information about a whaleship that may have been sailing out of this port in 1840."

"If it sailed out of this port anytime from Colonial days on, we have a record of it. What was its name?"

My throat felt constricted. What if I was about to learn that there never had been such a ship? "The *Unicorn.*"

"That strikes a bell. I'll look up the record to make sure. In the meantime, why don't you look at our scrimshaw?" He gestured at the glass-topped cases along one side of the room.

While he was gone, I moved from case to case, looking with as much interest as I could muster at lengths of whalebone long-dead whalers had incised with mermaids and full-rigged ships.

I was looking at the painting above the fireplace, an amateurishly stiff, but charming, portrait of a pantalooned little girl holding a white cat, when the curator came back into the room. Evidently he had made notes from the museum records, because he carried a piece of paper.

"Got it," he said. "The *Unicorn* was built by the Hampton Harbor Boatworks in 1833 at the commission of a Samuel Fitzwilliam, who according to the record owned several other ships." He glanced at the paper in his hand and then looked at me. "At the time you mentioned, 1840, the *Unicorn* was captained by a Jared Cantrell—What is it? Are you all right?"

"I'm fine."

"For a moment there you looked odd. Anyway, in July of 1840 Cantrell sailed the *Unicorn* to the South Pacific. After he

136

brought her home she must have changed hands, because according to the next entry, dated November, 1841, she'd acquired a new owner, one Jonas Ware, and a new captain, George Hobbs."

"You mean this Jonas Ware bought the ship from Samuel Fitzwilliam?"

"Bought it, inherited it, was awarded it in some sort of court action—the record doesn't say how he got it. Just that Ware became the new owner."

"There's nothing more in the record about Samuel Fitzwilliam?"

"That's all about him. But there's a little more about the *Unicorn.*" He glanced briefly at his notes. "She set out on her last voyage in 1850 and never came back. As happened quite often in those days, her crew sailed her into San Francisco Bay and then deserted her to join the California gold rush." He paused. "Was there something in particular you wanted to know about this Samuel Fitzwilliam?"

"A—a crime he might have been involved in."

"Oh." Evidently he was a sensitive man, enough so that he had become aware of my stress and was embarrassed by it. "Did you try the local press? I know our oldest newspaper didn't come into existence until shortly before the Civil War, but perhaps—"

"I tried the paper. No luck."

"The Village Hall?"

"I tried there too, and at the Criminal Courts Building in Riverhead. Nothing."

"Then I don't know—" He brightened. "I just remembered. I used to be president of the local historical society. We taped reminiscences of old timers. One of them was Medgar Wright, on Willow Street. He once mentioned to me that he had a whole stack of magazines collected by a great uncle, or maybe it was a great-great. The magazine was published in Chicago, and I gather it was kind of a *National Enquirer* of its day, except that it didn't concern itself with just current crimes and scandals. It printed accounts of crimes all over the world, as far back as those two little nephews Richard the Third supposedly murdered in the Tower. Of course, chances are that he didn't print what you're looking for. It would depend on whether or not what this Samuel Fitzwilliam did was—"

I never knew whether he had been about to say "grisly enough" or "revolting enough," because after a moment he added lamely, "It would depend upon whether it was of more than local interest."

"Thank you very much. Willow is one of those block-long streets running off Madison Street, isn't it?"

"Yes. You can't miss Medgar Wright's house. About fifteen years ago, after he turned sixty, he decided he was an artist. He keeps his art in his front yard."

I thanked the curator again and said goodbye.

A few minutes later I stopped my car outside a saltbox cottage of weathered brown shingles. Its front yard was filled, not unattractively, with growth that some might call weeds and others wildflowers, such as small white daisies and some even smaller pink flower I didn't recognize. The yard also displayed what I knew must be Medgar Wright's creations. A rusty bicycle with a metal pyramid, also rusty, resting on its seat. Several columns of blocks of wood nailed together at odd angles, each block painted a different color. An umbrella-type clothes dryer, with pieces of stained glass rather than laundry hanging from its extended arms.

At the top of a short flight of wooden steps a man stood on a kitchen step-stool, plying a feather duster to one of a row of metal mobiles dangling from the porch roof. At my approach he got down from the ladder and smiled at me. According to what the curator had said of him, Medgar Wright must have been in his mid-seventies, but his agility made him seem younger. So did the lively blue eyes set in a seamed, sun-browned face. He came down the steps to the walk, transferring the feather duster to his left hand.

"Good morning. The name's Medgar Wright."

"Gail Loring." We shook hands.

"Haven't come to buy one of my pieces, have you?"

"Well, no. Not that they aren't interesting," I added quickly.

"Everybody says that, but nobody seems interested enough. Not that I really mind. In fact, I've grown so used to my pieces that I'm not sure I want to sell them. Well, what does bring you here?"

I explained.

"So you think this Fitzwilliam may have been written up in one of Uncle Ken's magazines, do you? Well, he might have been. I wouldn't know. The stuff's never interested me. I just gave the magazines house room because I figure that they must be worth something, and so if I ever get really hard up— anyway, come in the house."

He ushered me into a dark-carpeted hallway and then, just beyond the foot of a narrow staircase, into a living room. I had expected to find his house filled with more of his art, but evidently he confined his creative efforts to the out-of-doors. The living room was commonplace, even dull, with brown wall-to-wall carpeting and upholstered furniture of a lighter brown. The only thing resembling art was a large colored photograph in an oval frame hanging on one wall. The subject was a young woman in a pompadour and a white blouse with a choker collar. Probably she had been Medgar Wright's mother. He resembled her.

"Wait here," he said, "while I go up to the attic. If I look through all the tables of contents it may take some time, so relax and read a magazine."

He disappeared. I sat down on the sofa, picked up from the coffee table a copy of *Newsweek,* and tried to concentrate on a movie review. Finally I gave that up and just stared through the thin window curtain at the mobiles twisting and turning as they dangled from the porch roof.

He was gone about twenty minutes. Then he returned, saying, "I found it." With what seemed to me reluctance he handed me a magazine with a yellow cover.

I had to force my gaze down to it. In Gothic letters, the words *Marlon's Monthly* were printed across the top of the cover. Just below it was the date of that issue: March 1, 1889.

Most of the cover was filled with a crude drawing of a huge man whose curly black beard hung almost to his waist. In each hand he brandished a long-barreled pistol. In one corner of the picture lay the crumpled bodies of one black woman and two men, one black and one white. In the lower part of the picture, kneeling before the bearded man, were a turbaned black woman and a white one. The black woman had raised clasped, imploring hands. The white one clutched a blanket-wrapped infant to her breast.

Across the bottom of the cover black letters said, "The Monster of Monroe Street."

My host said in a constrained voice, "Page eleven."

He was letting me know that he had read it. I liked him for not pretending that he hadn't. Hoping that the shaking of my fingers was not visible, I turned the yellow pages, found the story. Semiliterate and falsely pious, it was a good match for that crude cover drawing. It began:

"Back in the year 1840, lots of folks in Samuel Fitzwilliam's village must of thought he was a lucky man. His town, Hampton Harbor, N.Y., was a seaport, and he owned several fishing boats. He had a beautiful young wife and a child. He also kept slaves. Yes, folks must of called him fortunate.

"Yet verily, verily, I say unto you, no man is lucky once the devil enters his heart. And the devil entered Samuel Fitzwilliam's heart. For reasons no one ever knew, one night he turned a murderous rage on his own household. It is said that in his blood lust he murdered five or six human souls, including a young child."

The print blurred in front of my eyes. No, I thought. Oh, no! Not Charity.

After a moment my vision cleared. I forced myself to go on reading.

"As for Fitzwilliam's fate, it is lost in the mists of time. In those early days of the Republic, when many could remember George Washington, newspapers were few, and there were none at all on that sparsely settled end of Long Island. Records also were few, and often poorly kept. But stories were handed down. According to one such, Fitzwilliam finally turned his murderous fury on himself, shooting himself in the temple. According to another, he fled alone from the scene of carnage and was never apprehended. According to another, he took his young wife with him. But, Reader, we can be sure that God Is Not Mocked. If Fitzwilliam managed to escape the hangman's noose we can be sure that he fled to worse punishment. As long as he lived, he must have been tormented by the piteous cries of those innocents he slew."

For perhaps a minute after I finished reading I stared down at the page, too sick with horror even to look up. What utter trash, I told myself. This hack had sat out there in Chicago writing lurid articles without even bothering to check easily available facts. For instance, it was plain that he hadn't known Hampton Harbor was a whaling port. He had used the term fishing boats rather than whaleships.

But just because the writer was a hack, that didn't change the probability that his story in most respects was true. In fact, I was sure it was.

I forced myself to look up. "Thank you," I said, handing him the magazine.

He did not ask if Samuel Fitzwilliam had been an ancestral connection of mine. But I'm sure he had guessed that the answer was yes.

*T*wenty-one

❧

During the next two days I found I was living in a sort of limbo between worlds. I read from the several paperback editions of fiction and non-fiction books I had brought with me from New York. I watched TV on the old black-and-white set in the other parlor, the one that contained a sagging studio couch and a table piled high with dusty magazines. The TV had no cable attachment, and so all I could get were two Connecticut channels, but now and then they carried good programs. I grocery shopped, leaving my car in the supermarket parking lot rather than on the street so as to reduce my chances of encountering Martin. Not that by doing so I managed to keep him out of my mind. In fact, it was because of his comments about my thinness that I cooked several tempting and quite lavish meals for myself and managed to eat most of what I had prepared.

The furnishings of the rooms did not change during those two days, and the windows through which I saw early morning and sunset light did not shift around. And yet no matter how loud the power mowers or how numerous the jet trails criss-crossing, I never lost awareness for more than a minute or two of that other world of oil lamps and high-wheeled carriages and turbaned women in the kitchen.

And I never quite rid myself of the panic that had descended upon me that night I started to flee this house, only to find my way barred by what turned out to be my own shadow. I tried to ignore it, but it was still there, a little tomtom of alarm throbbing somewhere deep in my consciousness.

Twice during those two days I walked through the town's residential streets, narrow streets that meandered this way and that because—according to Miss Blaisdell—they had never been laid out "proper," but had followed the paths made by herds of cows and goats many years before the Revolution. I found that walking those streets was almost like moving through a living museum. I lingered before turreted and bay-windowed Victorians, and stately Greek Revival houses with pillared porches, and little eighteenth-century cottages with prim gossip benches facing each other on the small porches. And everywhere there were flowers. Roses spilling over picket fences. Hollyhocks standing against the gray wall of a two-hundred-year-old clapboard house. Riotously colorful beds of marigolds, zinnias, and snapdragons. And red geraniums in white marble urns on the lawn of a Greek Revival house.

Always, though, the thought of Martha Fitzwilliam kept me from any real enjoyment of these walks. I kept picturing how she must have passed along these streets, full skirts billowing around her. I thought of her pausing to admire some of these houses, not as stately survivors of the past, but as brand new additions to the town.

I visited Monroe Street. So far I had avoided even driving down it. But now, after parking my car, I moved slowly over the uneven old sidewalk. I passed five vacant lots, but realized that there was only the remotest chance that one of them had been the original site of my rented house. On none of them was there a crumbling foundation of the proper proportions, or any trace of the two slave cabins or the combined carriage house and stable.

I went to my car, parked under a willow tree whose roots had tilted a section of the sidewalk. I thought of something Martin had said. "Talk about feckless! Here the village's main street is lined with expensive street lamps of nineteenth century design. Yet all over town, sidewalks go unrepaired. That seems to be part of the charm of the place, though."

As I drove toward Converse Street I felt an almost irresistible urge to be with Martin and feel his arms around me, giving me at least an illusion of warmth and safety and happiness to come. But no. I'd had all that out with myself. I had no right to his love, or anyone's love. Not now, not yet.

As I was opening my front door, the phone began to ring. Sure who the caller was, I switched on the hallway light and then walked to the phone and picked it up.

Martin said, "Are you all right?"

"Yes."

"Only you're not, are you?"

"No."

"Won't you at least talk to me about it?"

"No. Not yet."

A long silence. Then he said, "Well, I thought there would be no harm in reminding you that I'm here . . . and hoping you'll call me."

He hung up.

I stood there, the phone in my hand. There was no change in my surroundings. The amber light globes still burned in their wall sockets. Across the hall a half-opened door showed me the round oak table and the octagonal glass light shade dangling above it. And yet, as so often happened, I felt a suddenly increased awareness of that other time flowing beneath the present.

And then I became aware, too, of that little tomtom inside me, beating a warning to get out—

And spend the rest of my life wondering just what had been my inheritance from the people who once lived in this house? No, that I wouldn't do.

144

I hung up the phone, went back to the kitchen, and cooked my solitary dinner.

During the night my subconscious must have worked on my problems, because when I woke up the next day, a Saturday, my first thought was: That church! The one where Samuel Fitzwilliam had been a deacon. What was the name of it? United Christian Brethren? Something like that. If the church were still in existence, it might have records dating back to Samuel's time.

I dressed quickly, went downstairs, phoned Miss Blaisdell. "Do you know if there is a United Christian Brethren Church around here?"

"Not now. All we got now are Catholics, Presbyterians, and Methodists. Oh, and a synagogue."

"You said, not now. How about in the past?"

"Oh, sure, only you got the name wrong. It was called the Brethren United in Christ. I know, because my mother told me how her grandmother used to belong to it. In fact, she and her husband fought over it regular. He was Presbyterian."

"What happened to the church?"

"The congregation, you mean? I guess they just dwindled down to a half-dozen or so. Anyway, they disbanded, oh, back before the Civil War. Don't know what happened to the building. Maybe they deconsecrated it and sold it to somebody who moved it away. Or maybe it just fell into ruins. Anyway, all that's left now is part of an old foundation. And the graveyard, of course."

My pulse leaped. A graveyard. More than likely it was there I would find Samuel Fitzwilliam's gravestone, if he died in this village.

"Where is the graveyard?"

"Right where the church was, of course, over in Northwest Woods."

"Northwest Woods!" I had seen the area marked on maps. "Why way over there? Wasn't that a long way for Hampton Harbor people to travel?"

"Yes, but the rest of the village wanted it that way. You see, the Brethren felt the Almighty really meant it when He told them to make a joyful noise unto the Lord. They made so much noise when they were here in the village that everyone complained. So finally they moved to Northwest Woods, where they could raise all the ruckus they wanted."

She paused, and then asked, "How come you're interested in the Brethren?"

"Oh, I've been reading this book about various sects on Long Island in the early nineteenth century." Before she could ask the name of the book, I hurried on. "Could you tell me just how to get to that graveyard?"

"Sure. Turn off the highway onto Silas Weemer's Path, then take the second road leading off to your left. And be careful you don't break an axle."

More than an hour later I realized what she had meant about breaking an axle. The road I followed was little more than two tire tracks, with weed-grown earth and an occasional fairly large rock between them. The road led through dense woodland. Overhead the branches of trees intermingled, so that I seemed to move through a greenish twilight.

I emerged into a clearing. If I had not known that once a building had stood there, I might not even have noticed what remained of the foundation, just a slight depression in the earth and, surrounding it, rocks and bits of mortar almost obscured by grass and low bushes.

The little graveyard was quite a different matter. Some person or persons had made it their business to keep up this lonely cemetery. Perhaps they had distant ancestors buried here. Perhaps they acted out of piety, or just love and respect for the past. But anyway, the picket fence, which must have been replaced a number of times over the years, sagged only a little, and recently had received a fresh coat of white paint. Any of the headstones which had toppled had been set upright. There even were flowers, not yet entirely withered, on two of the graves.

Heart beating fast, I went through the creaky little gate.

146

Half-an-hour later I came back through the gate to sit, defeated, behind the wheel of my car. I had seen gravestones ranging from that of an eighty-year-old man who had died in 1820 to that of a three-month-old girl who had died in 1858. But no headstone for a Fitzwilliam.

It seemed to me that made it almost certain. Samuel had managed to escape the consequences of his crime. He had fled somewhere and, heaven knew how many years later, had died and been buried there.

The day had become overcast. I knew I should go back and do some housework—clean the refrigerator, push the wheezing vaccuum cleaner around. The prospect seemed too depressing to face. What I wanted, suddenly, was to be with crowds of people. I drove to Southampton.

I found crowds, all right. Crowds in the Parrish Art Museum, moving through high-ceilinged rooms past paintings that ranged from Old Masters to Roy Lichtensteins. Crowds inspecting fashionable shop windows along Job's Lane.

When I started back to Hampton Harbor around six o'clock, I found traffic even heavier than it had been earlier that day. By the time I reached the house it was almost dark. The air, hot and humid all day, seemed to grow more so.

I left my car in the driveway of the rented house and went inside. Quickly I started up the stairs, eager to get under a cooling shower. When I was about halfway up the flight, I heard a heavy rumble of thunder. That was odd. Even though the sky had been overcast all day, there had been no hint of a coming storm. I climbed the rest of the stairs and started down the upper hall.

The nursery door stood open.

Charity must have recognized my step, because she called loudly, "Ma-*ma!* Ma-*ma!*"

Quickening my pace, I entered the nursery. She was standing in her crib, plump little hands fastened around its railing, small face wide awake in the soft glow of the nightlamp on a pine chest of drawers. I said, "Charity, you are a bad girl. You know you should be asleep. Why aren't you?"

She had seemed sound asleep only moments ago, when Flora had gone back to her quarters for the night and I had hurried next door to leave a crock of peach preserve on the back porch of our elderly neighbors, the Windsors.

Charity smiled and held out her arms to me. I knew I should not indulge her. Samuel had often pointed out that a parent should never reward a child's disobedience. But Samuel was not here. Around four that afternoon a boy from his office had arrived with the message that my husband would not be home for supper. Instead he would meet with a business associate at the Main Street Hotel. I had eaten my solitary meal at one end of the long mahogany table.

I reached down and lifted my little girl into my arms. How warm and soft she was! Her weight in my arms brought me consolation for the bleak knowledge that the *Unicorn* was to sail on the tide just before midnight. Eyes closed, I laid my cheek against her soft curls.

Another roll of thunder, closer now, and the first patter of rain on the roof.

Downstairs the front door opened and closed. Feet sounded on the stairs.

Samuel. I took a hasty step toward the crib. Then I froze, with my daughter still clutched in my arms. There was something ominous in his heavy and yet slightly uneven tread. Even before I saw him I knew that he had broken his long-held vow not to drink.

He stood in the doorway now. The upward-striking light from the night lamp shone on his curling back beard, his dark eyes looking larger and more lustrous than ever before.

Dear God, I thought. Samuel knows.

148

*T*wenty-two

❦

"Put the child down!"

His voice was so thick that it took me a moment or two to understand him. Perhaps in my alarm I had tightened my arms around Charity. Or perhaps the tension in the atmosphere, or the odor of whiskey, had frightened her. Anyway, she began to wail.

"Put the child down!"

"Please, my darling! Please don't cry." I lowered her onto her small bed. "It's all right."

Swiftly I bent and kissed my daughter, whose crying had quieted to whimpers. Samuel said, "Come with me!"

I straightened and followed my husband across the hall and into our bedroom. He closed the door. The faintest glimmer of gray light came through the windows, just enough that I could see him reach for the matchbox beside the lamp on one of the chests of drawers. Light bloomed, turning the window black. He whirled toward me.

"Whore. Jezebel. Adultress."

I made one feeble attempt at denial. "Samuel, I don't know what—"

"Keep quiet, madam. There's no point in trying to lie to me. It took days for the story to reach me, but tonight it did."

He paused, as if hoping I would try to say something, but fear held me silent.

"The man I had supper with at the hotel told me." Again rage thickened his voice. "He lives clear over in Greenport, and yet he'd heard."

Rain was pelting the window pane now. I managed to say, "Heard? Heard what, Samuel?"

"You and Jared Cantrell." His face was dark red now. "Cantrell, my best captain."

Apparently his throat had closed, because he fell silent for a moment. Then he said, "Up at the old fort. You with Cantrell, in broad daylight. You slut, you filthy slut.

"Don't try to deny it," he rushed on, even though I hadn't tried to speak. "You were seen."

I thought numbly, by whom? Some itinerant peddler who'd been camping out near the old fort? Some hanger-on at the livery stable where Jared had rented his mount? Something in Jared's manner might have aroused the idler's curiosity, enough so that he had followed—

Sickened, I thought of someone listening in the grove around the fort, or perhaps even silently climbing a tree to spy on us—

Lightning crackled, so close by that its glare was perceptible even in that lamplit room. A split second later thunder pealed. I whispered, "Samuel, what are you going to do?"

"Do? I shall put you from me, of course. Tomorrow Fergus will drive you to your parents' farm."

That farm fifteen miles away, where my two older sisters and I had grown up. It had been a poor sort of growing up. Oh, not because we lacked material things, although we did. It was poor because my parents were unloving people, who made no attempt to hide their disappointment that they had been denied sons to help till their few thin-soiled acres. My sisters, as soon as possible, had married sons of neighboring farmers. As for my own marriage, I think my parents regarded it as the one bit of

150

good fortune any of their children had brought them. I was seventeen, and Samuel was a widower of forty-three, but he was rich. They told me to marry him, and I did. How much money he gave them I don't know. I just know that while Samuel and I were still only engaged they bought several additional acres and a new team of plow horses.

It would not be pleasant, returning to a couple who every day would make me conscious of the bitter disgrace I had brought upon them. But there would be compensations. I would no longer have to fear that Samuel would someday visit his ill temper upon Charity. I would lie alone in bed at night. And—my heart leaped at the thought—when Jared came back, we would manage to see each other often. We could not marry, of course, not as long as Samuel lived, but I would have my beloved until the inevitable day when he turned to someone else.

I wanted desperately to know, but dared not ask, what Samuel intended to do about Jared. I did not have to ask, though.

Samuel said, "As for your paramour, I shall let him sail with the tide. I have too much invested in this voyage to delay it for days or even weeks while I search for a new captain. But when he returns he will learn that he has sailed for the last time on one of my ships, or perhaps any ship sailing out of Hampton Harbor."

Was he powerful enough to cause other shipowners to boycott Jared's services? Perhaps. But this wasn't the only port.

I waited until a clap of thunder rumbled away into the distance. Then I said, "Very well, Samuel. What time do you want me to leave tomorrow?"

"Sunup!"

"Charity and I will be ready."

"Charity! What does she have to do with this?" His astonishment seemed genuine. "Do you think for one moment that I would allow you to take my child with you?"

Terror squeezed my heart. As I looked at him, stricken dumb, he went on, "In such cases as this the law is unequivocal. You have thrown away all rights to our progeny. I shall send my daughter to Boston, where my sister will raise her."

His sister, his widowed and childless sister: I had seen her just once, at our wedding. Thinner than her brother, but with his cold, prominent dark eyes, she had chilled my spirit. And she would terrify Charity. At the thought of my small daughter being handed, helpless, to such a person, I began to scream inwardly.

Samuel said, "I shall make sure that my daughter has the most Christian of upbringings—"

"She is not your daughter."

His voice remained cold and even. "You do not know what you are saying. You are hysterical."

"She is not your daughter."

I saw the first terrible doubt come into his eyes. I said, "She is Jared Cantrell's daughter."

He stared at me. The fingers of his big hands curled, and I wondered if he wanted to feel them closing around my neck. He said, "Anybody would know that is a ridiculous lie. The child looks like *me*. That dark hair of hers—Cantrell's hair isn't that dark." He was gaining confidence. "Anyone can see she is my child."

"But she isn't." In another moment he might try to kill me, but right now I was the stronger. "When Charity was conceived you were up in Maine, supervising the building of your two newest ships. You were gone many months, remember."

"You whore, you lying whore. My child was conceived when I got back." Thunder cut off part of a sentence. "—born seven months later. She was born prematurely. Dr. Gothwaite told me so."

"Dr. Gothwaite lied to you. He lied for my sake and my baby's. It was the only way to save us."

And until now I had told no one, not even Jared. If he had known Charity was his he would have insisted that I come away with him, even though it would have meant that Charity would grow up shunned as the child of an adulterous union.

"You can't want her!" I cried. "Even when you thought she was yours, you didn't want her. We'll both go away, first thing in the morning."

Something in his congested face warned me. I had already opened the door when he lunged. I ran across the hall into the nursery, slammed its door, turned the heavy key in the lock.

Charity screamed. A lightning flash, mingling with the night-lamp's feeble glow, showed me that she was standing in her crib, face distorted with terror.

I said, just before the thunder rolled, "It's all right, my darling. It's all right."

Samuel's fists were thudding against the panels. "Open this door! Open it!"

For perhaps half a minute the thud of his fists mingled with Charity's crying. Then the pounding stopped. I heard him stride along the hall, start down the stairs.

Where was he going?

For a few minutes I could hear nothing but the drum of rain on the roof. Then I heard the distant slam of the back door.

I knew then where he was headed. That lean-to beside the carriage house.

In helpless panic I looked through the lamp's glow at my weeping child. The room was not a refuge now. It was a trap. He would come back, carrying one or both of those new acquisitions of his, Colt pistols which, once loaded, could fire six bullets. He would shoot off the lock—

But it would take time to load a pistol with bullets and powder.

I unlocked the door, swept my child into my arms, ran out of the room to the stairs. Where could I go for help? Not to the servants. Samuel was back there. As for our neighbors, the Windsors, they were not only old but quite deaf. It might take me many minutes to arouse them. And the neighbors on the other side of us had gone to Philadelphia to attend their son's wedding.

Best to hide in the house.

153

But where?

Not in the cellar or the attic. He would look in those places right away.

The closet under the stairs. He might never think of it. And even if he did open its door for a quick look inside, he would not be able to see us, not if we were hidden behind those stacks of hat boxes. There were articles back there—a dress form that had belonged to Samuel's first wife, a small chest, perhaps other things—but surely there would be room for us, too.

At the foot of the stairs I took a precious moment to open the front door wide. Let him waste time looking outside for us in the rain. Then I ran down the hall, dimly lighted by a lamp on the wall shelf next to the coat tree. I realized that my little girl had stopped crying. She was not even whimpering. I glanced at her white face. Plainly her fear had become so great that she could make no sound at all.

Cradling her in one arm, I opened the closet door, grasped the little wooden knob to close it behind us, heard the latch fall back into place. Now we were in complete darkness. "Please, my darling." From the shelf where Sara had placed the crocks a few nights ago came the faint smell of spiced peaches. "Don't make a sound, dearest. We'll be all right."

I put out an exploring hand, found the rear wall and the space between the wall and the stack of boxes nearest to it. The space was too small to squeeze through. With a cautionary whisper to my child, I put her down on the floor. Kneeling in the pitch darkness, I grasped the lowest box in the column with both hands and drew the whole stack forward a few inches. It did not topple. I picked Charity up, edged through the space I had opened, and again placed her on the floor. Then, holding my breath, and praying not to hear the opening of the back door and the tread of my husband's feet, I slowly drew the column of boxes back into place.

I gathered Charity close. Still not uttering a sound, she clung to me. Even in that closed space, I could hear the drum of rain

154

on the attic roof. Perhaps one or two of the boxes had toppled after all, the sound of their falling covered by the rain.

Don't think about it, I told myself.

The sound of Samuel's opening the back door must have been lost in a peal of thunder, because when I heard his running footsteps they were already quite close. They passed the closet door and then, a moment later, abruptly halted. He shouted something, and I knew he had caught sight of that open front door.

When next he shouted the sound was more distant. He was out in the rain now, searching for us. For the first time I wondered how I myself was to get out of the house. I would have to try to, sooner or later. If we stayed here too long, he was sure to find us. I had not thought of that when I carried my daughter in here. I had thought only of securing our immediate safety.

He was back in the house now, and running up the stairs. I heard doors bang and a piece of furniture, probably a straight chair, overturn. After that the sounds became distant and indistinct, and I knew he must be searching the attic. Then I again heard the pound of running footsteps on the stairs leading down from the second floor. As nearly as I could tell, he ran into both parlors and the dining room, shouting my name. Then I heard the latch lift and the door of our hiding place open.

I clapped my hand over Charity's mouth. Lamplight from the hall shone over that wall of empty boxes. If I had dislodged any of those boxes, there would be more than enough light for him to see it.

The dim glow vanished. The door closed. I heard his footsteps moving away. I took my hand from Charity's lips, and for the first time since I carried her down the stairs, she gave a whimper. "Sh-h-h!" I said, and the whimpering ceased.

He must have gone into the kitchen and lit a lamp there, because after a moment I heard the hollow drum of his feet on the cellar's wooden stairs. Despite the pounding rain, I could hear sounds from down there. Evidently he was moving boxes

155

and barrels about. Then he was back in the kitchen, back in the hallway—

I heard the back door open and slam shut.

Where was he going now? Had he decided we must have left the house? Was he going to saddle one of the horses and search the neighborhood?

In an agony of indecision, I clutched my silent child. If I left the house now, I might blunder into him. But if I stayed, he was almost sure to find us sooner or later. Even now he might have begun to think about that wall of stacked hat boxes in the stair closet.

Minutes passed. Clinging tightly to me, my little girl remained silent. I wondered if she would remember anything of this night, and what such a memory might do to her.

Sounds. The back door opening. Voices. A number of people moving along the hall. I heard Fergus say, "It is a late hour for the wee bairn." I heard my husband answer, "I won't keep him or any of you awake for long."

He sounded quite sober, as if all that running about through the rainy night had dissipated the liquor fumes in his brain. Whatever he did next, whiskey could not be blamed for it.

The wee bairn, Angus had said. His and Flora's little son, the child that, because of Samuel's open resentment of him, they had placed with relatives. I recalled now that the child had been brought that afternoon to spend Saturday night and then the Sabbath with his parents. A new dread, as yet nameless, stole over me.

They passed the stair closet. It sounded as if he had brought all the servants into the house. Why? And what had he told them? I realized then that he need not have told them anything except to come with him. They were his property—the blacks until they died, Fergus and Flora for another four years. If they disobeyed, he could inflict corporal punishment. If they ran away, the authorities would return them to him, just as they would a strayed horse.

Was he carrying those Colt pistols? And if so, did they know it? Or were the weapons hidden by his coattails?

The rain must have let up for a moment or so, because I could tell that they had gone into the west parlor. I heard the door close. I even heard the heavy key grate in the lock.

And then I heard the loud, haranguing voice, the words, obscured by a renewed assault of wind-driven rain. I thought, with everything inside me tightening up, he sounds far worse than drunk. He sounds mad.

Perhaps he had always been mad beneath that tightly controlled exterior of his. Perhaps the revelations made to him tonight—that Jared and I were lovers, that Charity was Jared's child—had caused that madness to burst its bounds. Unable to find its real target, my child and myself, that madness was venting itself on the rest of the household. Perhaps he suspected, rightly, that at least some of the servants had known about Jared and me.

I heard a scream—Sara's?—and then a shot, and then more screams, and a man's hoarse cry, and more shots. I heard a shattering of glass, as if someone had tried to escape through a window, and then a small child's cry, and more shots. Charity was sobbing in my arms now. Sick with horror, I made no attempt to quiet her.

Silence descended, broken only by the drum of rain and by Charity's sobs, now diminishing to whimpers. After that terrible uproar, the silence seemed not just an absence of sound but an entity in itself, swelling out of that parlor and into the rest of the house.

I held Charity close and listened. Still no sound except the rain. A vision of that parlor rose before me. The sprawled, motionless bodies. Shattered glass. Blood. And in the midst of it, slumped in a chair or stretched out on the floor, gun still in his hand, the lifeless bulk of the man to whom I'd been married for almost eight years.

I had to get us out of this house. True, he might not have killed himself, might be waiting for me to emerge from our hiding place, but I had to get out. I whispered, "Be quiet for a little longer, my darling." Then I eased us past that stack of boxes, groped in the darkness until I found the latchstring. I opened the door and ran on tiptoe down the hall to the back entrance.

*T*wenty-three

❦

As we emerged into the night, Charity hid her face against my breast. Rain deluged us, falling into my eyes and making it even harder to see through the darkness. I ran around the corner of the house, skirted the north wall. Ahead the parlor windows cast lighted rectangles onto the drenched grass. Sickened at the very thought of looking through those windows, I ran past the house and across the front lawn to the sidewalk. I turned to my right on the sloping street.

Charity was crying again. "Yes, darling," I said. "Cry all you want to now. You'll be safe soon." Safe aboard the *Unicorn*. Safe with her father.

I ran on down the wet sidewalk, praying that my feet would not encounter a broken spot or slippery leaves. Always I was straining my ears for the sound of horse's hooves or running human footsteps behind me. If I heard anything, I had decided, I would dart into the rainy blackness between two houses and hide. But I heard no sounds of pursuit.

Despite my sense of deliverance, horror and grief still weighted my heart. Grief for Sara and Callie and Hannibal, those three who had been to me not just domestics but friends. Grief for the McClintocks, who would never have the rewards they had hoped to reap in their adopted land once their seven years of bondage were over. Most sharply of all, perhaps, I felt grief for that other child, that handsome little boy, born in this country and with every possibility open to him, who now almost certainly lay in a small, lifeless heap back in that parlor.

And then terror drove everything else out of my mind and heart. The beat of horse's hooves, back there somewhere in the rainy dark.

So Samuel hadn't shot himself. Instead he had left his victims and resumed his search for Charity and me. He must have looked into that cupboard, finally, and seen dislodged hat boxes, and guessed that had been our hiding place. And now he was coming after us. I cursed the faint-heartedness that had kept me from looking through the parlor window to make sure that he had turned the gun upon himself.

The house just ahead was dark. No time to run up onto the porch and try to arouse its occupants. But despite the wind-lashed rain, I could make out the big oak tree on the lawn. I ran through the drenched grass and, holding tight to my little girl, pressed close to the rough tree trunk.

Then relief turned me weak. Through the pound of hooves I heard another sound, the squeak of wheels. Samuel wouldn't have taken the time to hitch up any sort of vehicle. Nevertheless, I waited a few moments before I peered cautiously around the tree trunk.

Dr. Gothwaite's buggy passed at a smart clip, with the doctor's dark bulk in the driver's seat. He had a passenger beside him, someone small. Eight-year-old Elijah Foster? Probably the latest of the Foster brood had chosen this storm-drenched night to enter the world, and young Elijah had been dispatched to fetch the doctor.

The buggy passed. A moment later I realized that I could have called out. But no matter. I did not have much farther to go. I recrossed the lawn to the sidewalk and ran on.

Out of breath, and with pain growing in my side, I turned onto Main Street. Streetlamps shone on rain-lashed sidewalks that were almost empty, although light and male voices and sometimes the sound of singing filtered through the closed windows of the grog shops we passed.

As if sensing that we had almost reached safety, Charity had fallen silent. I stepped onto Long Wharf's rough planking. Here, despite the rain, dozens of men moved about, wheeling barrows and casks and boxes aboard whaleships, unwinding lines from hawsers. Looking neither to the right nor left, I was nevertheless aware of their scrutiny.

Jared's ship was the last in the line of vessels. Flaring torches on its deck showed me the unicorn figurehead. Unable to hold up my skirt because of the child in my arms, I stumbled near the top of the gangplank and might have fallen if someone had not reached out to grasp my elbow. I saw that he was a middle-aged man in wide homespun trousers and a whaleman's short jacket.

I gasped out a thank-you and then said, "Where is Captain Cantrell?"

He gave me a gap-toothed smile. "I'll show you, ma'am."

I followed him down a companionway. He stopped at a closed door. "Here's his quarters, ma'am," he said, and walked back toward the deck.

I knocked. "Jared! Jared!"

He opened the door, his look of delighted astonishment giving way almost instantly to one of concern. He was in shirtsleeves. I could see his officer's coat behind him, hanging from a hook on the wall.

"Martha!" He drew me inside, closed the door. "What is it? No, wait a minute. Catch your breath."

With Charity still in my arms, I sank onto the edge of his bunk bed. I had a vague impression of my surroundings. The oil lamps in their gimbals. A desk with an open ledger—the ship's log?—resting upon it. The chair he must have pushed back when I knocked.

I said, "Samuel—went crazy. Oh, God, Jared! I think he's killed them. Sara and Callie and Hannibal and the McClintocks and their little boy, all of them, maybe himself too."

I saw the leap of horror in his eyes. His voice, though, was quiet. "Tell me from the beginning, if you can."

"He—he shot them because he couldn't find Charity and me. I'd hidden from him. You see, someone had told him about you and me—"

I broke off and then said, "He was going to send me back to my parents. That I was just as glad of. But he was also going to take Charity from me and give her to his Boston sister to raise. And so I told him the truth."

"You told him what, Martha?"

"That Charity wasn't his. She's yours, Jared. When Samuel came back from that shipyard in Maine, I'd already been expecting for two months. You were someplace off South America by that time, of course. You didn't come back to the Harbor until Charity was four months old."

An almost incredulous joy had leaped into his eyes. He looked from my face to that of the exhausted child in my arms. "But why? Why did you never tell me?"

"I didn't dare. If you'd known, you'd have moved heaven and earth to make me leave Samuel and come away with you. That might or might not have meant ruining your career. But certainly it would have meant a lifelong stigma for Charity. When he said he was going to take her from me, though, I realized that almost any sort of life would be better for her than being raised by that terrible woman."

Jared bent down, took Charity gently from my arms, and laid her on the bunk. She stared up at him, no longer afraid, but pale with exhaustion. Jared drew me to my feet.

We stood in close embrace, his lips on mine, his hands warm through my rain-soaked dress. Then he said, "You'll both sail with me tonight. I'll leave you with my cousins down in Virginia—"

Someone knocked. "Cap'n! Cap'n Cantrell!"

162

Jared opened the door. I saw the same gap-toothed man who had helped me come aboard the ship. His avidly curious gaze went to me and then back to Jared.

"News about the owner, Cap'n. Somebody just brought it."

"All right, Thompson. I'll come up on deck." He closed the door, reached for his coat. "Wait here, darling."

He came back in a few minutes. "It was the constable's young brother who brought the news. It seems that the old couple next door, the ones you've told me about, heard the gunshots even though they are quite hard of hearing. For a while they were afraid to do anything at all, but finally the husband went to the constable's house and told him.

"It's just as you thought," he went on. "He killed the others and then turned one of the pistols on himself."

I drew a shuddering breath. He said, "Since he was my employer, I had best go up there, and talk to the constable. But the ship is ready to sail with the tide. Now take off that wet dress, my darling, and then get under the blankets. I'll—I'll try to get you another dress before we sail."

When he had gone I looked down at my daughter. She was asleep. Her lashes lay like dark fans on cheeks that had been deathly pale less than half an hour ago. Now color had returned to her face.

I took off my dress and hung it on a hook near the one which had held Jared's coat. My camisole and my outer petticoat were damp, but my corset and my inner petticoat were quite dry. I lifted my sleeping child, drew back the blanket on which she lay, and then spread it over her. I lay down beside her.

That dress Jared would try to bring me. He wouldn't take one from my own wardrobe, not with the constable apt to ask questions and perhaps try to hold up the sailing of the ship if he guessed I was aboard it. That left about only one place where a seafaring man could find a woman's dress at this time of night. My dress would be supplied by an inmate of one of the port's several bawdy houses.

No matter. I would have a dry dress to put on in the morning when the *Unicorn* would be sailing down the Atlantic Coast, each moment leaving that house on Monroe Street farther behind, each moment bringing nearer the life I would share with Jared.

Underneath my fatigue and my sense of horror, I felt a stubborn upwelling of something else, an eager joy.

I closed my eyes. I had intended to stay awake, but I felt myself sliding into sleep, there beside my slumbering child.

*T*wenty-four

❦

Abruptly I found that I sat behind the wheel of my rented car. It stood near the far end of the wharf, out where a century-and-a-half ago broad-beamed whaleships had rocked gently at their moorings. Although the night was humid, there was no evidence that any rain at all had fallen.

At the other end of the wharf, where it joined Main Street, figures moved about in the glow of an arc light. I looked at my luminous-dialed watch. Eleven-fifteen. The Wharf Club was open by now. Those people down there must be young teenagers, beer or soft-drink cans in hand, milling about in front of the club they could not enter.

With a calmness I myself found amazing, I thought: So my great-great-great-grandmother had no drop of Samuel Fitzwilliam's blood in her veins. How strange to think of that terrified little girl even as a mother, let alone a grandmother several times over. Did she ever learn she was Jared Cantrell's child? I rather doubted it. Or, if Martha had told her after she reached a certain age, she must have pledged her daughter to secrecy.

Martha, after all, was an early Victorian. She'd had to choose whether her child would bear the stigma of bastardy, or of being the lawful offspring of a man who had committed a monstrous crime. My guess is that, to Martha, the latter would seem preferable. And so—Charity, down there in Roanoke or wherever Mr. and Mrs. Jared Cantrell settled, must have grown up believing that her father was her stepfather. Jared must have hated that. But also, loving Martha as he did, he must have been happy to have her and their child on any terms.

And so the garbled and fragmented story of Charity's frightful heritage had filtered down through the generations—until one afternoon on the porch of a rundown beach cottage in New Jersey, my great aunt had passed it on to me.

I knew now that I would never have been able to find the record of Samuel Fitzwilliam's trial. There had been no trial. As for his grave, he had committed suicide at a time when those who died by their own hands could be denied burial in hallowed ground. Certainly a literal-minded sect like the Brethren would have denied him such burial. If I searched long and diligently—which I had no intention of doing—I might learn where the local authorities of that day had placed his body. Probably it was in some cemetery miles from Hampton Harbor.

Sara and Callie and Hannibal were quite a different matter. They might have been buried in the graveyard of the African Methodist Church out on the county highway, a cemetery I had passed several times. Tomorrow or the next day I might drive out there and search for their headstones, although I doubted that their stones, if indeed any had been erected, would still be standing.

As for Fergus and Flora and their small son, it seemed likely to me that their "up island" relatives who had cared for their little boy had claimed the bodies and buried them in a cemetery in their own village.

Again I thought of Martha and Jared, sailing southward toward their joined futures. I hoped that theirs had been long lives and more than ordinarily happy ones. And I realized that the sense of joyous freedom the thought of them brought me was not chiefly for them. It was for myself.

Underpinning my other fears—fear of the alcoholism in my family, fear that again I might have to enter a place like that clinic—underneath those fears had been the illogical one implanted in my mind when I was eleven years old: the fear that something dark and twisted, something inherited from a man long dead, might manifest itself in me. Now that I knew there was not the slightest possibility of such an inheritance, my other fears too slipped from me. As Martin had said, almost any family includes a couple of drunks. And as my doctor at the clinic had said, almost anyone, no matter how normal, will break if stress becomes too great. But it's not apt to happen twice to the same person, she had told me. In fact, many patients emerge from the breakdown stronger than before. I found that now I could believe that.

I got out of the car and walked back along the wharf, skirting the group of teenagers in front of the club. To assert their manhood, several of them whistled at me. In my giddy exuberance I thought of whistling back, but didn't.

On this Saturday night in July, Main Street was as crowded and lively as it must have been in whaling days. There were no Fiji Islanders with bones in their noses. No grog shops. No drunken combatants rolling in the gutter, while a crowd of spectators yelled encouragement in English, Portuguese, and several American Indian tongues. But there were hordes of casually chic young people moving in and out of bars, or gathered in groups on the sidewalk, or leaning against Jaguars and BMWs parked at the curb.

I reached the real estate office. With a leap of gladness I saw that the windows of the apartment above were still lit. I climbed the stairs, knocked.

Martin opened the door. In one hand he carried a book, with his forefinger marking his place. He said, "You're about the last person I expected to see. Come in, come in," Then, "My God! You look wonderful."

167

"I am." I laughed. "I don't mean that. I mean I feel wonderful. What's the book?"

"Elements of Deconstructionism. The friend who's saving his seminar notes for me recommended that I read it."

"What's Deconstructionism?"

"Don't ask. You really wouldn't want to know." He laid the book on a coffee table before a plump sofa covered in black-and-white ticking. "Now tell me why you feel wonderful."

"You really wouldn't want to know *that,* although I suppose I'll tell you sooner or later. All I'll say at the moment is that the Monster of Monroe Street who lived a hundred and fifty years ago has nothing to do with me. I know that now."

He bent, took my face in his hands, and kissed me soundly. "That's what I've been telling you. I also told you—or did I—that I wouldn't care if you were descended from Ivan the Terrible. Come here."

He sat down in one corner of the sofa and drew me down beside him. Half sitting, half lying on the long cushion, I leaned back against his chest. He clasped his arms loosely around me. "But do me a favor," he said. "No matter how you feel now, get out of that house."

"I intend to. Tomorrow I'll move to a motel. Maybe after a few days you'll be able to find a room or apartment for me."

"That would take some doing." His arms tightened around me. "But what you could do is move in here with me for the rest of the summer."

After a moment I twisted around so that I faced him. "I could, couldn't I?"

He gave a huge smile. "You *have* changed." Then he kissed me, long and enthusiastically. Then I again rested my head against his chest. He said, "We'll go over there and get your gear first thing in the morning."

"Okay."

His right hand had begun to stroke my arm, left bare by my tee shirt. There was something familiar about that particular caress. Something familiar, too, in the look of his hand, with its long fingers, and with the hairs curling on his wrist. Hairs that glistened, not in July sunlight falling into a ruined fort on a long ago afternoon, but in the lamplight of this room above the noisy Main Street of a resort town.

Could it be? Could it be that the last time around—or maybe the time before that—he had been handsomer, shorter, a man who made a living hunting whales rather than lecturing college freshmen about Milton?

It was an idea I found both interesting and pleasant. Even though I knew he would scoff, I might tell him about it some-day.

But not tonight.